# Betrayal

*A Regency Romance*

BY

# Jaimey Grant

copyright © 2008 Laura J Miller
cover art © 2009 Laura J Miller
All Rights Reserved. No portion of this work may be reproduced in print or electronically without the written permission of the author.

ISBN: 1440414688
EAN-13: 978-1440414688

First published in September 2008
Second edition

The following is a work of fiction. Any similarity to real persons, living or dead, is purely coincidental.

# Betrayal

# Chapter One

*London*
*Early December 1816*

The once beautiful young woman slumped against the cold stone of her prison cell, her knees drawn up to her chest, her tattered skirts pulled carefully down to cover her skinny limbs. She wondered if she would ever be free. It seemed no matter where she went, no matter how she changed her appearance, she was always found. Then, to avoid starving, she had stolen a measly loaf of bread and ended up here.

Newgate.

The very name was enough to strike fear into most human beings. But some were so desperate for food they took the risk to feed themselves and their families. Anyone unlucky enough to get caught faced deportation or worse, hanging.

Some actually viewed deportation as the worst of the two, but this young female prisoner was infinitely sorry she had been sentenced to hang instead. If she were deported, even as a criminal, she would have been able to finally escape those that pursued her, forget about her past, and start a new life.

She shivered and pulled her threadbare shawl tighter around her painfully thin body. It was very cold in her cell since prisoners of her kind did not rank high enough to warrant a fire or any type of comfort. What was the point? They would all die eventually anyway.

She almost laughed at the consternation that would quickly run through all those faceless men who had decided her fate if they were aware of who she was and exactly what position she held in the *haute ton*.

But she wouldn't tell them. They wouldn't believe her, of course, if she did tell them, but they might ask her family, who would reply with great breaths of relief that she had stubbornly run away and they had been searching for her this age. Then they would let drop that she was quite mad and cite several instances where she had appeared to be so. She would be handed over and locked up in a madhouse, where they said she belonged.

She would never go back there. She would die first.

And all this over a few measly pounds and paltry title she didn't even want.

Perhaps it wasn't a few pounds, she thought as a shuddering cough wracked her frail body. Sixty thousand a year made her one of the richest women in the country. The title wasn't paltry either. There were very few women in England who could claim a title in her own right. But it was all very useless when there were several titled family members swearing to your insanity and doing everything in their power to lock you away. If she were proven mad, the family would have control of her money until the day she died, although the title would remain hers until that time.

A guard passed her cell and leered in at her and she knew it was only a matter of time before he had his way with her. She thought about it in a detached sort of way, by this time too jaded to really care and having lost her virtue long ago, she knew she was damaged goods, unmarriageable, so it didn't matter. In cynical Society, if one man had had you, you might as well have given yourself to all of them.

And to avoid starvation, she had very nearly done just that.

She would have thought that her looks had gone off enough that she would not have to worry so much about being molested. Her red hair was dull and cut ruthlessly short by an inexpert hand causing it to fall in limp dirty strands all around her gaunt face, her skin was sallow and scarred, her figure had gone from seductively curved to miserably skinny, and even she knew that she smelled something awful having not had the luxury of soap and water for quite some time. The only claims to beauty that she seemed to have retained were her large green eyes, which still flashed with anger or mirth depending on her mood, and her deep bosom.

She reflected ruefully that of all the attractions she could have done without, her breasts were it. Breasts seemed to cause thoughts of lust in even the most staid of gentlemen, no matter their age, station or current marital status.

If she had had less spirit and less pride—and if the threat to her life had not been quite so great—she could have become some man's mistress and lived her days out in comfort. Even though red hair was considered quite unfashionable, this particular lady was undeniably beautiful.

Was, past tense.

Now she looked like any hungry waif off the street, grimly awaiting the fulfillment of her sentence. It would be a release, she thought with resignation, suddenly not caring that they would hang her just so long as she didn't have to hurt anymore.

She was so tired of running. She was tired of making friends only to have to leave them when it became too dangerous. She was tired of casting furtive glances over her shoulder fearing she was being followed.

She was tired of wishing that a certain gentleman were looking for her because he cared and not because her family had asked him to do so.

She heard the key grate in the lock and wondered which of the poor souls around her would go next. She didn't turn to look at the man who owned the heavy tread but she dimly noted that he came her way. She just assumed it was the guard come to take his pleasure of her then turn her over to her fate.

"I had the very devil of a time finding you," muttered an annoyed voice very close to her ear.

She turned her head wearily and smiled in defeat at the exceedingly attractive and very perturbed gentleman that crouched next to her. "What took you so long?" she asked conversationally. "Come to watch me dangle, have you?" She laughed bitterly and turned away, not wanting him to see the tears that unaccountably sprang into her eyes.

The very elegant Adam Prestwich wrinkled his nose fastidiously. "Faugh, you smell abominable!"

"And where, my charming sir, do you suppose I would get a bath? I can hardly trade my favors for hot water and soap when any man here can have me without going to so much trouble. I am the lowest bloody form of human life: a poor female criminal with no one to protect her," she replied candidly, still not looking at him, her voice thick with sudden grief over her sorry lot in life.

"You speech is abominable as well. One would never know that you were once a lady. Or that you hold one of the oldest titles in the land," her companion growled roughly.

Adam Prestwich looked at her with chilly gray-green eyes. She couldn't read his thoughts since the man was so damn good at concealing them. But she knew he was not pleased to see her here.

"Why are you here?" she finally asked.

"Stand up" was his terse reply.

She obeyed since it was quite stupid to argue with any man when you were little better than a trollop and a thief and condemned to die. On the other hand…she was going to die.

When he turned away and commanded her to follow him, she balked.

"Go to hell," she replied equably, a wraithlike smile twisting her thin lips. Some of the other female prisoners sniggered and one cackled at her to go with the swell and—the rest was better left unsaid.

He didn't bother trying to convince her to go. He picked her up, slung her over his immaculately clad shoulder and marched from the cell. She pounded on his back ineffectually and finally attempted to kick him in a very tender area. She received a hard swat on her rump for her pains.

"Behave or I will take you back and let you die, brat."

"Then take me back!" she retorted angrily.

He didn't reply so she lapsed into furious silence, trying to block out the vulgar remarks and catcalls that followed them every step of the way from the prison.

She knew he would return her to her family. She didn't know why. She had been running from this particular man for years now. He was determined to find her and return her to the bosom of her "loving" family. She wondered what sort of Haymarket scene of tender filial devotion he had been treated to.

The cold night air hit her like a hammer blow. Mr. Prestwich walked down the street and she wondered crossly if he was planning to walk all the way to Lancashire to deliver her to a fate worse than death. She began to shiver uncontrollably from cold, exhaustion, and long suppressed emotion.

They stopped suddenly and she was bundled into a closed carriage. Mr. Prestwich laid her on one seat with the utmost tenderness and covered her carefully with two heavy rugs. His solicitation frightened her more than if he had beaten her to within an inch of her life. Every traumatic thing in her short life converged on her in a rush of intense emotion and she fainted for the first time.

Adam watched her in the dim light thrown from the carriage lamps. He was surprised he had recognized her under all her rags and layers of dirt. How the devil had she ended up on the street and hungry enough to steal? It was sad to see a once pert and beautiful woman brought so low.

Which only made him wonder yet again what had kept her running. He had met her family and they seemed all that was proper in a loving family that feared for the safety of the runaway heiress. He was cynical enough to realize that it probably had more to do with her title and inheritance than any altruistic motives on their parts. But he had to wonder at the sanity of a girl who would rather hang as a thief than try to cope with even the worst of relatives.

The carriage swayed gently over the rough cobbles of London. Gaslights on the street shined in through the open windows of the conveyance highlighting the deathly pallor of his companion and he wrenched the curtains closed. It was unlikely that any members of the *ton* would see them at this time of the morning, but he didn't want to take any chances.

The coach eventually turned into Berkeley Square and came to a stop before a mansion in Berkeley Street. Adam opened the trap and called up to the coachman.

"Go around to the mews, John. I want to go in the back."

The coachman said nothing about this rather odd request but everyone knew the Quality had strange ways about them. Hadn't he just driven his very elegant master to Newgate where said master had returned with a woman of skin and bones? John Coachman grunted, the trap banged shut and the coach moved on.

They stopped again and Adam leaned forward, gathering the unconscious girl in his arms. She didn't move and for one brief panicked moment, he thought she was dead. The thought caused a strange twinge in his heart, which he put down to travel fatigue. He had searched practically the length and breadth of England for this particular quarry, always avoiding London since it would be damned stupid of her to enter the metropolis, and he was deuced tired. He was also annoyed to finally find her where he had never thought to seriously look.

He climbed down from the carriage and peered closely at her in the growing light of dawn. The air had a metallic taste, heralding forthcoming snow.

Her face was deathly pale, her eyes sunken in her head, and her lips were an alarming shade of blue. She suddenly inhaled and a ragged cough wracked her whole body.

He cursed as he strode swiftly into his mansion. He supposed he could have taken her to his friend's wife, Lady Verena Northwicke, but that lady had only recently given birth to twins and Adam had already brought her enough grief with his groundless accusations and petty spite. No, he would have to look after Lady Brianna Derring, Countess of Rothsmere—better known as Bridgette—himself.

# Chapter Two

Bri awoke slowly, unaccountably warm and with a feeling of security. She wondered what caused this since the last thing she remembered was awaiting her fate in Newgate Prison. She opened her eyes slowly and looked around—and encountered carefully blank gray-green eyes set in a harshly handsome face.

"Adam!"

Her voice was a mere croak of sound and she found a glass of water thrust at her with a terse command to drink. She obeyed since she really had no other choice. After a moment, she tried again.

"Where are we?" she whispered.

Adam shifted restlessly in the hard chair by the bed. Why the deuce were bedside chairs always so blasted uncomfortable? It made no sense.

"We are at Lockwood House in Berkeley Street."

She gave him a look of confusion. He watched the look pass over her once beautiful features and again experienced that odd pain in his chest. He shook it off, attributing it to indigestion this time.

"My townhouse," he supplied woodenly.

She seemed to lose even more color, as if that were possible. "We're still in London?"

"Of course we are. Your family is here."

Her eyes widened until they were great green saucers in her gaunt face. She seemed to be struggling with some strong emotion.

She was. Rage. She wished she had the strength to claw his eyes out. She wanted to slap that sardonic look off his face. She wanted to plant him a facer. She wanted to kiss those lips that were now curling into a mocking grin.

Oh, Lord! She must be delirious. She couldn't possibly want to kiss him. He was despicable. He was little better than a Bow Street Runner. Actually, he was worse. He hunted innocent humans purely for the thrill of the chase.

"I think I'm feverish," she mumbled thickly. She did feel awfully hot. And her body positively ached.

Adam reached over and felt her forehead. She was almost too hot to touch. He had to get a doctor, but there was no one he could trust. He wanted to find out from her what was going on before handing her over to her family. He hoped it was nothing too bad since he had to turn her over, no matter what. She was only twenty. She still had nearly five years before she gained complete control of her inheritance.

He suddenly thought of Connor. It was very early, but he knew his friend would come.

He stood up and rang the bell. Mrs. Campion arrived a moment later.

"Mr. Prestwich?"

"Sit with Miss Bri, Mrs. Campion. I have to ride for a doctor."

The motherly housekeeper curtsied and took Adam's seat by the bed. He reflected irrelevantly that she seemed quite comfortable in the cursed chair from hell. He turned on his heel and left.

Charger, his great black hunter, stamped and pawed at the ground as if sensing his master's agitation. The beast was soon saddled and pounding through the London streets. Adam reflected as he rode that the snow he had suspected had made its appearance a trifle sooner than he had at first thought. Thankfully, it wasn't yet a detriment to his horse or himself as he raced to Vale Place at breakneck speed.

Adam thanked God that Connor had seen fit to come to town for a brief stay. Verena had given birth to twins, a boy and a girl, less than two months ago and so was unable to travel to the metropolis with her husband. But Connor, now the Marquess of Beverley although he refused to the use the title for personal reasons since the death of his brother, had some necessary business to attend to and so had left his young wife at Denbigh Castle, his childhood home.

Adam reined in as Vale Place came into view. The impressive residence, located in Grosvenor Square, was deceptive in appearance. It appeared small and quaint on the outside; inside was like a veritable palace.

Tossing the reins to a footman who came hurrying out, Adam

burst into the house. The butler, Samson—an old man with long white hair tied neatly at his nape—bustled forward.

"Get Lord Connor at once. Tell him it's an emergency." He turned to the footman still on duty. "Have my lord's horse saddled immediately." The lad jumped to do his bidding, all the servants knowing that Mr. Adam Prestwich was as near to being the second master at Vale Place as any man ever could be.

Samson moved faster than Adam could ever remember him moving. Deciding to wait in the hall, Adam moved towards the chair that leaned against the wall. He eyed it with a cynical light. Good God, he was to be plagued with hard chairs for the rest of his life, he thought.

"What's to do?" Connor asked as he came down the stairs, shrugging into a brown riding jacket.

"Glad to see you dressed for riding," Adam remarked as he headed back to the door.

Connor followed with his normal easy-going complacence, being long used to his friend's strange quirks. When they reached the horses, Adam suddenly turned to him.

"Damn! Get whatever you need to cure a raging fever. I have need of your doctoring skills."

Connor raised one pale brow in question, but said nothing and sent the footman to retrieve some items for him from the kitchen.

Then they were off, rocketing through the deserted city streets as if being pursued by Satan himself.

Adam paused outside the door to Bri's room, stopping so suddenly Connor almost bumped into him. The marquess threw his friend a startled look that held a twinge of amusement and waited patiently for Adam to explain whatever freakish start now held him.

Prestwich looked back at Connor assessingly for a moment, a shadow crossing his chiseled features. His friend cocked an eyebrow inquiringly but said nothing.

"Before I let you through this door, I must demand absolute secrecy about the presence of the person in this room," Adam finally uttered into the lengthening silence.

Connor nodded in agreement, his curiosity and the shiver of unease he suddenly felt hidden underneath a calm façade.

"Especially your wife. Verena can't know," Adam added

emphatically, finally looking his friend in the eye, his hand poised above the door handle.

His eyebrows threatening to disappear into his hairline, Lord Connor agreed. Other than his initial look of surprise at the odd request, he was careful to conceal his feelings behind a serious tone and a bland expression.

Satisfied with his friend's answer and demeanor of seriousness —Connor never gave his word lightly—Adam nodded and turned the handle on the door leading to his unwilling guest. "Follow me," he said unnecessarily. His tone was resigned as if he would have much rather kept the countess's presence a secret—which, of course, he wished with his whole heart were possible, but he knew, at this point, that it couldn't be helped.

Adam gave his housekeeper a speaking glance. She bustled from the room, giving Lord Connor a friendly smile as she went.

"Bridgette?" Connor uttered in disbelief, keeping his voice low as he stared at the familiar face in the bed.

"Brianna, actually," Adam replied helpfully, advancing a little further into the room. He shrugged and met Connor's eyes, a half-smile twisting his lips at the look of bewilderment on the marquess's face. "Well, to be completely accurate and strictly proper, my lady the Countess of Rothsmere," he added dryly.

Shocked blue eyes met wry gray ones for a moment before swiveling back to the emaciated form in the huge four-poster. Connor shouldn't have been as surprised as he felt at that moment. He distinctly recalled a certain thought he had had about Bri over a year ago. He had suspected even then that she was Quality.

"I assume you will explain," replied Connor with a frown, his composure restored with the usual rapid recovery for which he was known. His voice held a note of unmistakable command seldom if ever heard in the easy-going young lord.

Adam responded to it the same way that he would have responded to anyone unwise enough to order him to do anything: "No."

"I'm not giving you a choice, Adam" was the firm reply.

Connor stared at his friend and didn't move from his place just inside the open door.

Adam remembered that look from when they were children. Connor rarely was serious but Adam Prestwich knew better than to simply ignore him when he was in such a mood. He wanted answers and when Lord Connor Northwicke wanted answers, that was exactly what he got—even if he had to use his fists to get them.

Despite Adam's being taller and heavier, Connor was virtually unstoppable in a fist fight, as Adam had cause to know having seen any number of bullies bested by the younger—and often smaller—man. Adam could see he wouldn't fare any better if he persisted in being stubborn.

Not that he was afraid of him.

"Very well," Prestwich conceded grudgingly. "I will tell you if you help her and promise to keep quiet about everything."

"Should I be insulted?" Connor asked with the ghost of a smile on his face. "You seem to have little faith in my discretion."

"Devil take you, it isn't that," Adam retorted sharply. He searched for a reason for his unusually unguarded tongue. "If anyone finds out she's here, she'd be compromised and I'd be forced to play the part of a gentleman and marry the chit," he said in a low growl, praying his tone was convincing enough to throw Connor off.

"Why?" the marquess asked simply. "You could always let her face the scandal alone, you know."

Adam stared at his best friend in genuine disbelief. "I think I've just been roundly insulted but you have a funny way of telling a man he's less than a gentleman."

Moving into the room, Connor stood beside the bed and looked down at the young woman who had posed as his wife's abigail just over a year ago. It was amazing the change time and most likely unspeakable hardship had wrought.

Looking up at Adam who stood at the end of the bed, he inquired mildly, "And you trust your servants to keep such a delicious *on dit* to themselves? One of the wealthiest heiresses in the land pretending to be what she is not and residing under the roof of a suspected rake. I'm tempted to spread the word myself. Do you realize how popular I'd be with such a scandalous piece of gossip? I'd be feted and petted wherever I go."

He was obviously teasing, but Adam had to suppress a desire to wipe the smile off his friend's face with his fist. "Of course I trust my servants," he replied instead, completely ignoring the rest of his friend's words. "Every last one of them is loyal to me and knows it would be more than their lives are worth should they dare betray me. Besides, they are unaware of her true identity."

"Would it be so bad to marry her?" Connor asked then, abruptly changing the subject back to what he felt was the true issue. "You have to get married sometime, you know."

Connor turned away to prepare to examine the sleeping Bri and so he missed the flurry of emotions that flashed across Adam's features. When he regained his composure, the older man offered nonchalantly, "I do? Whatever for? I can leave my wealth to whomever I deem worthy and I have no title to pass on."

"Do you not?"

# Chapter Three

Adam stared. Connor ignored his friend and rang for Mrs. Campion. Then he turned and explained, "It might be best to have a woman present."

"What do you mean by that?" Prestwich finally snapped.

Easily following his friend's train of thought, Connor retorted with a slight twinge of heat, "Just what I said: Do you or do you not you have a title to pass on? I realize the title of baronet is not much compared to a duke or a marquess or even a baron for that matter, but it is a title nevertheless and should be handed to someone worthy." He paused, but not long enough for Adam to reply. "As it was to you," Lord Connor concluded in a gentler tone.

"How the bloody hell did you find out?" Adam exploded right as the housekeeper made her entrance after a minor scratching on the door—a good servant never knocks.

She stopped in her tracks and looked from one gentleman to the other warily. A soft moan issued from the bed and Connor glanced at Bri quickly before returning his attention to Mrs. Campion. He bade her enter and put her at ease with a friendly smile. He explained quickly what he expected from her and she resumed her seat near the bed.

Connor swiftly and efficiently examined the countess in a very impersonal manner while Adam retreated to the peace and sanity of his library. He needed a drink, he thought even as he poured a stiff measure of brandy. He started to set the decanter back in the cupboard, hesitated, and then, after retrieving a bottle of port from the cabinet as well, carried both back with him to a cozy leather armchair by the fire. He placed the liquor on a table beside him within easy reach and quaffed the amber liquid already in his glass.

He refilled it, drank it down, and refilled it again before he finally started to relax. He sat with the glass in one hand and stared beyond the chair's twin out into the lightening gray sky of early morning. God, how he wished this day was over. Or better yet, had never happened.

What the devil had ever possessed him to take up such a ridiculous hobby?

Even better question: How the devil had Connor discovered that he, Mr. Adam Prestwich, was in actuality *Sir* Adam Prestwich? A reluctant part of him had to admire his best friend. It wasn't something the man just stumbled over. He must have had some sort of inkling and decided to investigate. With Adam's own interest in discovering certain facts that were nigh impossible to uncover, he couldn't help but be impressed by Connor's triumph.

He just wished the bloody marquess had chosen a different... victim on which to practice his rapidly maturing sleuthing skills.

Adam had gone to a lot of trouble to bury the fact that he was a baronet. He sincerely believed that he didn't deserve it no matter what Wellington and Prinny said about the issue. It was moot that he had no use for titles anyway. The power behind the aristocracy seemed to be blown all out of proportion with some of the highest titles in the land being held by greedy, vulgar, licentious, and sometimes downright evil men. He had no desire to be numbered among them.

His glass was filled a fourth time but this time he only sipped at it. He was tempted to empty the bottle and perhaps two or three more after that. Thinking about his title only made him think about his past and...her.

He shook his head as if to clear the thought from his mind. He would not think of the lying, greedy little witch. He would not!

He decided his military career, which had started out so promising, was the start of his real bitterness, and yes, even hatred in regard to the fair sex. Had he not begged Connor's father, the Duke of Denbigh, to help him get into a good regiment, he would never have had to endure the pain of the past two years.

The war with Napoleon had escalated and Adam had a desire to see if he could help rid the peninsula of the Corsican monster. The duke was more than willing to assist him and confided to Adam that he wanted Connor to go as well. Connor had refused pointblank when asked, much to everyone's astonishment. It was indeed odd that the bookish Adam was determined to go and the sport-loving Connor absolutely refused.

He had arrived in time to participate in the battle of Vitoria in 1813. That battle had more or less decided the fate of Napoleon.

Wellington's victory at Vitoria had rallied the Prussians and even contributed toward the reentry of Austria into the war against France.

Adam's performance at Vitoria resulted in his promotion from lieutenant to major. By the time the battle of Toulouse ended and Napoleon was abdicated to the island of Elba, Adam had risen to the rank of colonel. That was a title of which he could be proud.

Being by now drunk enough to conveniently forget the difficult time between the time of Napoleon's abdication in April 1814 and his subsequent escape in March of the following year, Adam thought about his injury at Quatre Bras. He wasn't actually supposed to have been where he was at the time. His inner demons had driven him to stand anywhere on the field where he might die —which actually could have been anywhere.

As it turned out, Adam Prestwich was blessed—or cursed, from his viewpoint—with the luck of the devil. He was struck down, shrapnel lodging deep in his thigh. It ended up being a very minor wound. He had contracted the inevitable fever, however, and found himself on the next ship to England right after the battle of Waterloo and the end of Napoleon's illustrious career. Even the fever neglected to kill him and spare him from the pain of living.

He was awarded the baronetcy for showing bravery on the field of battle. Bravery, hah! He was the veriest coward. He was only on the field praying for death and his plans had gone awry. Hence, his reason for refusing to acknowledge his title.

"Drowning your sorrows?" asked an amused voice from the now open door.

Adam shrugged. Well, he tried to. He was far more intoxicated than he had at first supposed. When he moved his shoulder in a gesture that was as natural to him as breathing, his head swam alarmingly and the whole room tilted.

He clapped a hand to his head to steady it. Unfortunately, it was the hand that held his half-empty glass. Brandy sloshed over the edge and down his black hair, down his unshaven cheek, and onto his white waistcoat. A few drops even managed to land on his buckskins.

"Bloody hell," he muttered—slurred, rather. He glanced at the decanter beside him and realized it was empty. As was the bottle of port. Damn. When had that happened?

"Let me help, old man," his friend said good-naturedly as he removed the glass from Adam's hand and mopped up most of the mess with a large handkerchief. "I wager you haven't slept in days." He rang for Adam's batman, Morris. The valet entered, took one look at his master, and groaned—loudly.

"The devil!" Prestwich ground out, much to the amusement of his friend and servant. He glared at both of them. "Get out!"

The valet was known for never speaking. The occasional sound would slip from between the man's thin lips, but not very often. It seemed to suit Adam and Morris nicely to converse without actual words. Now the valet took Adam by the arm, heaved the much larger man out of the chair, and simply led him away.

Connor watched them leave with the same amused smile in his eyes. As soon as the door closed, however, the smile disappeared and what Connor Northwicke felt then was far from amusement. He hated the situation that Adam had embroiled him in and he hated even more lying to Verena. He was definitely not looking forward to the scene that would ensue when she found out. And find out, she would. It was inevitable.

The Countess of Rothsmere. Hers was an old and powerful family full of dukes, earls, and viscounts. Connor thought there was even a baron in there somewhere. He wondered what had caused her to run away from a revered title and riches beyond anyone's wildest dreams. It had to have been quite bad. Connor wondered if Adam had considered this. He wondered if Adam would go through with returning her to her family. With Adam, one never really knew what he would decide.

Lord Connor walked over and reached into the cupboard by the desk, removed another bottle of brandy and poured himself a glass. He quaffed it, set the glass on the desk, and left the room.

He popped his head into the sickroom and murmured a few short orders to Mrs. Campion. Then, after a moment of indecision as to whether or not he should leave something for the massive hangover Adam was sure to have later in the day, Connor shook his head and left the third floor.

As he donned his despised hat—he hated hats, always had—his gloves, cloak, and took up his riding crop, Connor thanked God fervently that Verena had not accompanied him to Town this time. At least he had some time to prepare for the coming battle.

# Chapter Four

Prestwich came awake with a pounding headache. His mouth felt like carpet and his stomach protested vociferously every time he moved so much as a hair. He wondered with a detached feeling if he was dying. It was quite the worst hangover he'd ever experienced.

He wondered why. Drink had never affected him so violently before. Then he remembered. When one neglected to eat and then filled that empty belly with spirits, it was like drinking twice the amount actually consumed. His brow furrowed. How could he have forgotten to eat?

And he had forgotten...all day, all night, and the entire day before. Blast! He forced his eyes open and blinked in the glare from the light streaming in the window facing his bed. Where was Morris? The man knew how Adam hated light when he felt so damned sick.

"Morris!" he bellowed.

That was stupid.

The shout reverberated through his head, threatening to crack his skull. He squeezed his eyes shut and prayed for death. Unfortunately, all he got in answer for his heartfelt prayer was wretchedly sick in the chamberpot next to his bed.

A few minutes later, he smelled the distinct aroma of coffee. He also smelled something sickeningly sweet and yet as putrid as the streets of London on a sultry summer day. It was familiar and he realized with a twinge of dread that it was Morris's infallible cure for a hangover. It tasted as disgusting as it smelled and Adam did not look forward to taking it. He wished Connor had had the decency to leave something for him. But he knew his friend well enough to know that the marquess would think it would serve Adam right for getting so tap-hackled. Morris's cure was more punishment than relief.

The smell of the blasted stuff was making him want to cast up his non-existent accounts again. He wondered a trifle illogically if he would end his days by literally puking his guts out. Was it possible?

He found a glass shoved in his hand and had to swallow convulsively to avoid being sick again. Adam glared at his silent valet, who had the nerve to look back with a cheeky smile as if amused by his master's imminent passing. As soon as the coffee cup was drained, Adam blessedly passed out again.

Two and a half hours later, Adam was feeling much better, once again sure that he would live. He was on his way to see his guest and find out how she was doing. He doubted very much that the fever had broken, but he wanted to see for himself that she was resting peacefully.

She was. In fact, she was sleeping so peacefully, a shiver of alarm snaked up his spine. Maybe she was dead. He approached silently and was relieved to see the subtle rising and falling of her chest beneath the blankets. A fire crackled merrily in the grate casting a warm glow over the room. The drapes were drawn to keep out the late afternoon sunlight. Mrs. Campion was dozing next to the bed.

The housekeeper came awake when Adam released the deep breath he'd had no idea he was holding. Stammering out apologies for having fallen asleep, she rose to her feet, bobbing a curtsy as she did so. Adam assured her that she needn't worry about it.

"You are doing more than could be reasonably expected of you," he said mildly. "Why don't you appoint a maid to sit with her while she sleeps?"

The woman's eyes grew worried for a moment. "I would, sir, but they are such flighty creatures. I feel more comfortable watching over her myself."

"So be it," her master replied with a shrug. He couldn't recall having ever hired a flighty maid and he was sure his redoubtable housekeeper would not but he really couldn't be worried about servant matters at the moment. "Has there been any change?"

"No, sir. She awoke a few moments ago and I gave her the powders just like Lord Connor showed me. Then she went back to sleep."

"Has she been able to eat anything? And keep it down?"

The woman frowned. "No, sir. That is, she drank some broth,

but she couldn't keep it down."

Adam was worried. He thought her inability to retain sustenance was due more to the near starvation she had suffered rather than the fever itself. He had no doubt that when the time came to really try to overcome that, he would need Connor again.

"Has she spoken at all?"

Mrs. Campion—the Mrs. was a courtesy title—scrunched up her doughy face thoughtfully. "She mumbled something about not letting, um, you, sir, take her back. Then she sighed and said... love, no, Levi? Yes, Levi. That was it."

"She didn't say anything else?" Adam asked a trifle shortly.

"No, sir, that was all."

"Very well. I have some things to do. I'll return to see how she goes on before dinner."

Adam left the house in a bit of a temper. She was dreaming of another man. How dare she think about someone else when... When what? Why the devil was he so upset? He sounded almost... jealous.

Heaven forbid, *was* he jealous? He didn't even like women; he certainly wouldn't be jealous if one should show a preference for someone other than himself. A woman only served one useful purpose he could think of and that was best served flat on her back. Beyond that, he had no use for them.

He shoved the thought of jealousy aside. He realized with dismay that he was nearing Hyde Park and it was the time of the promenade. He hated the promenade.

It was not as busy at this time of year. For one thing, it was too cold for most. It was also too early for the height of the Season. There were not nearly as many people in Town.

But even with the drastically dissipated numbers of human beings in London, someone always stopped to talk to him; débutantes flirted, hopeful mamas tried to draw him into conversations extolling the many virtues of Miss This and Lady That, gentlemen tried to claim more than a mere acquaintance with him, etc. It was vastly annoying.

"I say, Prestwich, are you back in Town?"

Adam reluctantly brought Charger to a halt. The great black beast stamped his feet in irritation. He was brought swiftly under control and stood placidly enough while his eyes darted around looking for...a victim, most likely.

Adam resisted the urge to reply with the obvious rejoinder "Of course I am, you bloody nodcock" and said instead, only a trifle sarcastically, "As you can see." He left it at that and made to move on. This was generally enough to discourage conversation.

Evidently, Lord Hubert Baxter was either completely oblivious or else had no fear of dying. He reined in closer to Charger, who took exception to the movement and tried to rear up. Adam kept his seat and barked a sharp command at the horse. The large beast quieted instantly, satisfying himself with an angry snort while he pawed at the thin layer of snow covering the ground.

"I heard you were in the north recently, Prestwich," Baxter said then, his keen eyes missing nothing.

Adam looked at the once handsome, now scarred visage of the lord. He could barely tolerate the man in the best of moods. He was not in the best of moods now. "I was," he answered curtly, hoping his obvious disinterest in anything Baxter had to say would bring an end to the conversation.

It seemed his famous luck had run out. "And who kept your ladybird company while you were off gallivanting across the country?" the lord asked insolently.

This was the other reason he hated the park. Unless there was a lady present, Adam was always inundated with questions about his mistress. Everyone eagerly awaited the moment it was known that he let her go and some other lucky gentleman had the chance to be her protector. He actually considered sending an announcement to the papers to save a lot of people a lot of trouble when…if…the time came.

As much as Adam disliked women and sometimes hated them, he had been with his mistress since his return from the peninsula. He found her interesting as a person and, although he wouldn't admit it even to himself, she was far more than a mistress. She was his friend. He wasn't bored with her yet although it had been well over a year since he'd met her and she had agreed to be his mistress.

She was also, unfortunately, an actress at the Theatre Royal in Drury Lane. Worse than that, she was an exceptional actress of exceptional beauty. She was a great favorite with the gentlemen and the green room was always full to overflowing with her admirers, often men who wanted no more than a glimpse of the exotic beauty.

She was Miss Raven Emerson, The Ebony Swan.

It was her role as Juliet that made her really famous. She *was* Juliet. She made every audience member feel her blossoming awareness of first love, her desperation to be with her love despite all odds, her despair and confusion over her cousin's death at the hands of her love, her sudden loss and anguish at her dearest Romeo's passing, and ultimately, her own release in death.

It was not very often that true beauty and natural talent converged in one person on the stage but Raven was that perfect entity. She was tall—only a head shorter than Adam who was over six feet tall. Her hair was glossy black, straight, and silky. She never wore it up, not even at home. She had dark, nearly black eyes that tilted slightly giving her an exotic look. Delicately arched brows and long black lashes made her eyes stand out even more than they normally would have. Her nose was in perfect proportion to her face and her mouth was made for kissing with a fuller bottom lip and a slightly thinner top one. She was naturally graceful in movement and with every spoken word she managed to captivate man and woman alike, even her fellow actors.

Adam knew he was not the only man who found her appearance irresistibly seductive. Baxter had been after her since before Adam had even known of her existence. Raven had confided that the man was one of the few gentlemen who accosted her regularly that refused to take no for an answer.

Adam had never cared whether or not she was faithful to him, but he had always had the feeling that she was. Even Baxter's words failed to rouse his anger with Raven. It did, however, rouse his anger at Baxter. Prestwich was tempted to call the man out and have done with the whole damnable situation.

"I imagine she kept herself suitably entertained. And since you ask, she was obviously wise enough not to have been with you," he said equably. "And now, I really must go."

# Chapter Five

Raven kept rooms near the theater for convenience sake although Adam knew she had the wherewithal to buy a house if she wished. His offer to set her up in a quaint little house on the outskirts of Town had been turned down with a smile and assurances that she was quite comfortable right where she was. She was frugal with her money and unlike most courtesans, she knew the wisdom of saving for a rainy day, or in her case, her retirement from the theater. He admitted to a reluctant admiration of her because of this.

He walked into her little sitting room where he knew she would be at this time of day. She usually practiced her lines there with the help of her little maid, Molly. He waited patiently until Molly was dismissed before he approached the actress.

Raven smiled at him, delighted to see him, as usual. He wondered if she ever thought he might marry her. She had never in any way indicated that she felt he should or would, but how was he to know what actually went on in the woman's head? She was, after all, a woman. Didn't they all cherish hopes of matrimony?

When she saw the look on his face, Raven took his hand and led him out and up the stairs to her bedchamber. She normally did not like to indulge in sexual activity so close to the time when she had to be at the theater, but she sensed in Adam the need for a release and she was more than willing to oblige him.

He had, after all, been the one to introduce her to the fine art of lovemaking. It had been against her earliest decisions to take a protector. But that was before she learned of the unpredictability of receiving her pay for working at the playhouse.

And that was before she had met Adam Prestwich. He had not attempted to turn her head with the empty flattery that she so often received from other gentlemen. But the admiration was clear in his eyes and for the first time she had found herself sorely tempted by a man.

It had only taken the first time he asked her to be his mistress and she had heard a voice remarkably like her own saying yes.

That had been well over a year ago. She had been an actress since she was twenty. Even at that young age she had a wisdom beyond her years. She had at one time carried the hope of meeting and falling in love with a man who would marry her and save her family from penury. A year of trying to make ends meet on her meager salary with ten other mouths to feed had changed that. But she found she was unable to bring herself to say the words that would seal her fate with some gentleman who was only interested in her body and not her heart or mind.

But in Adam she had sensed a need. What it was, she wasn't sure. But it was there nonetheless, and she was willing to try to learn what it was he needed and strive to meet that need.

And now, she thought of him as her closest friend.

An hour of pleasurable activity later, Raven half-dozed in the circle of Adam's arms. They lay on their sides facing each other and he held her against him while wondering when he would get bored with her. He was amazed at how long he had been with her already.

Normally, he gave a mistress her marching orders after a relatively short acquaintance. He remembered the longest as being about two months. They always seemed to become rather arrogant and sure of his affections. One had even had the gall to ask when they were to be married. After dropping her unceremoniously on the floor—he had been in the process of carrying her up to her bed—he had sworn never to have anything to do with semi-respectable ladies of the *ton* again. That was one promise he had found relatively easy to keep.

He had never wondered or particularly cared what went on in any woman's mind, much less a whore's. But he often found himself pondering the inner workings of Raven's beautiful head and sometimes even asking her.

Perhaps he did this because he had trouble really thinking of her as a whore. She had been innocent until the first time with him and he had been strangely flattered that she would choose him for her first sexual experience even though he knew she had had several offers from half the gentlemen of the *beau monde*. Surely, she could have found a man far better heeled than he was and far more handsome, definitely far more personable?

But she had chosen him and as much as he tried to tell himself that she was just like every other woman—a scheming little adventuress just trying to get her hands on as much wealth as she could—he was never truly convinced of what to him was a fact rather than mere conjecture.

Black eyes opened and gazed sleepily up into his. He hadn't even realized he was staring at her. She smiled and kissed him lightly on the lips. When he didn't smile back, just continued to look at her intently, she asked, "Is something wrong, Adam?"

He liked her offstage voice. She had a soft, slightly husky voice that he found soothing and erotic at the same time. He traced the line of her jaw with one long finger and kissed her deeply.

Just before rolling her onto her back and covering her body with his, he whispered, "I'll tell you later."

It was some time later that Raven finally had the answer to her question. Well, *an* answer at any rate.

They were once again in the position of him holding her, only this time he was lying on his back and staring up at the silk canopy of the bed. She was laying half on top of him, one hand playing idly with the dark curling hairs on his chest and one leg draped negligently over both of his. He had drawn the bedsheet up to cover the lower half of their bodies. Both were relaxed and smiling.

They lay like that for several minutes before Adam recalled her question.

"Did you really want to know if something was wrong?" he asked with a slightly cynically inflection in his voice.

She cuffed him lightly on the chest. "I would not have asked if I didn't want to know," she replied with a smile that took the sting out of her action.

He had to smile. "I have a problem," he began, his smile disappearing as he thought about Lady Rothsmere.

Raven waited patiently, knowing Adam would only continue when he was ready. When he rose and dressed, she sat up, a little puzzled but still silent.

Pausing with his hands in the middle of tying his cravat, he said reflectively, "I find myself encumbered with a certain burden who refuses to...cooperate."

This was enough to arouse Raven's curiosity. Rising and pulling on a robe, she asked, "Can I help in any way?"

Gazing at his beautiful mistress thoughtfully, he nodded.

"Perhaps." Glancing at the clock on the mantle, he smiled. "We are both late now, my dear. I am due at White's and you should be at the theater."

"You look awfully pensive, old man. What's to do?"

Adam didn't bother to rise. He simply gestured to the seat opposite and waited for Connor to sit down.

"Nothing is wrong except I have a runaway heiress in my house and a sick feeling in my stomach that she would actually be better off with me than with her own family."

"I wondered if you had realized," Con said seriously. He ordered from the waiter that approached and sat silently until the man had left before continuing. "I have to admit that I wonder what would make one of the richest titled ladies run away and actually prefer to be left to die as a petty thief in Newgate. She must have been desperate."

"Or out for a lark that went desperately wrong?" Adam inserted cynically.

Connor considered that for a split second before firmly shaking his head. "I think some investigation into her family is called for, Adam. Her actions are too extreme. Even for a woman of her stubborn hardheadedness."

Agreeing reluctantly, Adam added, "If they discover I'm back before I learn anything, I will have to return her. I can't legally hold her. She is underage, Con."

The subject seemed closed for the moment. The friends ate steadily for a while before Connor cleared his throat and said, "I have to go back to Denbigh soon."

Adam's fork paused *en route* to his mouth. He set it down on his plate and pushed the plate away. "How soon?"

"I wanted to leave tomorrow."

"You can't," Prestwich returned bluntly.

"I can't?" His tone was disbelieving.

"No, you can't. What if something happens to Bri? I can't take care of a feverish countess who hates the very sight of me. What if she dies, Con?"

"That's your own fault," Con retorted. "Her hating you, I mean. As for the rest, I can wait only a few days. I will leave as soon as her fever breaks. After that, you will have no problem."

"She was starving."

"I know. It wasn't hard to tell."

"She can't keep anything down. What if she still dies even after the fever breaks?"

By now, Adam could hear the worry and desperation in his own voice. And he hated it.

"After the play tonight," Con replied in a seeming *non sequitur*, "we will go to the green room and visit your friend the Swan."

"Why do you—"

"Trust me," Con interrupted forcefully. "Don't worry." He rose to his feet and prepared to take his leave. "Come around for me at half past seven if you will. Until then."

# Chapter Six

The Theatre Royal in Drury Lane that evening was crowded despite the lack of Society in Town. Hundreds of candles blazed in large chandeliers poised above the full pit below. Even the boxes were crowded with those members of the *ton* who either stayed in London all year or were there on some business or other.

Adam and Connor were of the latter group. Connor preferred to spend his time in the country with his wife and children and Adam had never found London very interesting when Parliament was not in session.

The play started and Adam marveled anew at the beauty and grace of the lead actress. She *was* the play. Everyone else were little more than props to accentuate how very perfect she was. He watched her closely, a look of pride on his face.

The actor playing the role of Romeo was a young man almost too beautiful to be a man but he played his part well. Adam was nearly convinced that he was in love with his companion. And Raven...well, she was everything a young girl in love should be. Radiant, joyous, and yet despairing that she would ever be able to declare her feelings to all and sundry.

The play duly ended and Adam found himself in the green room bowing in front of Raven. She gave him a welcoming smile and offered him her hand.

When Connor approached, her smile grew. "Lord Connor! I was not expecting you. How is your wife?"

Connor engaged in a few moments of small talk with the actress. Then, "I have a favor to ask, if you would allow me a few private moments of your time."

Biting her lip, she had to ask, "You are not going to ask me to be your mistress, are you, my lord? As flattering as the offer is, I am quite taken."

Connor almost thought she was in earnest. Then he caught the amusement in Adam's eyes. "I am heartbroken, indeed, Miss

Emerson. However, that was not exactly what I was interested in discussing."

She threw a puzzled look at Adam who returned it with one of his own. "How can I be of service to you, gentlemen?"

"I understand you have some experience with nursing sick persons," Connor said. It was not a question.

"Nursing, my lord? Why, yes, I do. My father was sick for many years before I finally journeyed to London. I helped my mother take care of him until she died and then it was I who nursed him for a time with the help of my sisters."

Lord Connor appeared satisfied. Adam had a sinking feeling in the pit of his stomach. What the devil was the other man up to?

"Good. I have need of your services."

"Just what the devil are you doing?" Adam asked then in a fierce whisper that was actually pointless since Raven was standing right in front of him and could hear every word anyway.

Giving his friend a look of supreme annoyance, he said, "You have a patient whom you desperately need to keep secret. Miss Emerson would never dare gossip about the situation."

Returning his attention back to Raven, he asked, "Are you willing to see my patient and attempt to help in any way you can?"

Raven looked from one man to the other, her dark and perfectly arched brows drawn down in a V of confusion. "I suppose I can meet your patient, but beyond that I cannot promise anything."

Adam listened with mixed feelings. On one hand, Connor had a point. Raven would be the perfect candidate for such a position. She would help Bri to the best of her ability while keeping her mouth firmly shut. Society might be unhappy with him bringing his mistress into what was more or less his family home, but Society could go hang for all he cared.

On the other hand, Bri was a countess. Despite her past, she should not be subjected to the company of a kept woman.

With that thought, Adam glanced at Raven and immediately changed his mind on the last point. Raven was more of a lady than Brianna, Countess of Rothsmere. Bri's past put her beyond the pale.

Realizing he was being stared at, he nodded once.

"Would tomorrow afternoon be too soon to meet her, my lord?"

"Perfect," Connor replied with a smile. "Three o'clock?"

She nodded.

"Shall I send a carriage to you tomorrow?" Connor asked quietly.

"Yes, thank you," she replied, dismissing them as regally as a queen.

Adam spent an unusually sleepless night, tossing and turning, unable to get comfortable. His mind whirled with thoughts of his guest, worry over her health and sorrow over her actions.

Rising earlier than was his wont, he visited his ward, found nothing to have changed, and sequestered himself in his study to catch up some much neglected paperwork. When the hour neared three, he rose and relieved the housekeeper of her post at the countess's bedside.

His expected guests arrived promptly and were shown into Bri's room. He rose to his feet and greeted them stiffly before retiring into the corner to await the outcome of Raven's meeting with her potential patient.

They spoke in hushed voices by the bed as Connor explained everything that was wrong with the countess and the treatments he recommended. He listened attentively to any opinions or questions Raven had and offered his own in return. They were both very professional. Mrs. Campion returned and joined them there, adding her two pennies worth with a confidence Adam had never before seen her display.

It was at the very moment Connor turned to say something to him, Adam, that Bri awoke.

"Adam?"

Her voice came out as a pathetic croak and Adam rushed to her side. He picked up a glass of water and sat down on the bed beside her. He slid one arm beneath her and gently lifted her so she could drink. She still felt hot to the touch but she seemed to be coherent at least. He hoped it was a good sign. It had to be. The thought of her dying caused a distinct and very uncomfortable pang in the region of his heart.

"Adam?" she said again, a little stronger but still a pathetic whisper.

"I'm here, Bri," Adam said softly, still holding her up. She let her head fall against his shoulder and he set the glass aside. He brushed a few strands of dark red hair from her face.

"I'm scared," she admitted with a catch in her voice. A strange feeling of protectiveness welled up inside of him at her faintly spoken confession.

"I'm here," he said again as he held her against him and stroked her hair.

He remembered the way she was before. She had been vibrant and beautiful, full of life and willing to fight anyone unwise enough to set her off. She had proven to be quite a formidable prey to track and he had always secretly admired her fortitude and inner strength. He hoped she was physically strong enough now to beat the illness holding her. It would be a sad loss if she were to die.

She was soon asleep and Adam became aware of his surroundings once again. He looked up into the amused face of his best friend and the blank expression of his mistress. He wondered what she was thinking. He knew what Connor was thinking. And Adam very much wanted to hit him for it.

Laying the countess gently back into her bed and tucking the covers up around her, he turned to glare at Connor and Raven. The former grinned back and the latter offered a hesitant, fleeting smile as well.

"So are you willing to help, Miss Emerson?" Connor asked the actress then.

"It is up to Adam, I think, my lord. It is his home after all and his…secret."

Her voice had very little of the husky note it usually carried and Adam became aware for the first time of her appearance. She wore a dark blue wool gown of very modest—one might even say strict—cut with long tight sleeves and a high neckline, although the waist was up around the armpits as fashion dictated. Her hair, that glorious mane of shining black silk, was pulled severely away from her face and actually gathered into a knot, *a knot!* at the nape of her neck. She still had the seductively exotic eyes but with the severe hairstyle, she appeared a little less like she'd just emerged from a bedroom after a particularly energetic session of lovemaking. She looked so very professional, less like an actress and more like a governess.

Except for her lips. Her lips were made for kissing and she would never be able to escape that fact.

Perhaps Bri need never know that her nurse was an actress?

"Very well," he capitulated with a slightly mocking bow. He turned and left them to their plans.

# Chapter Seven

She came awake slowly. She heard a husky but decidedly feminine voice coming from somewhere far off to her right. The voice was asking her how she felt and if she wanted some water.

Water, yes. Bri opened her eyes and tried to nod. She felt her body lifted and a glass was pressed to her cracked lips. The water was cool and tasted subtly of barley. She must be sick, she thought suddenly. What happened?

The glass disappeared, she was laid back against the pillows and she turned to ask the voice where she was and what had happened. The owner of the voice had gone, however, and she was forced to wait.

She felt tired and achy all over but her mind was restless. She drew every ounce of strength she possessed into her arms and back and resolutely pushed herself up to rest her head weakly against the headboard.

She must have dozed lightly because she suddenly became aware of voices speaking quietly together right beside her.

"You didn't lift her up?" said a male one sharply. Adam, she knew.

"No, I didn't. She must have done it after I left to fetch you." It was the husky feminine voice again. She sounded quite amazed and Bri felt very proud of herself for accomplishing such a mundane feat as raising her tired body up.

"Does she have the strength to do that?" Adam again, incredulous this time. Bri felt unaccountably hurt by his disbelieving tone.

"I don't see how she possibly could," replied a wondering third voice, male. She recognized Verena's husband, Lord Connor.

"I think she's waking up." The woman this time. Amusement was rife in her voice.

Bri swallowed hard and opened her eyes. She must have moved in some way to indicate she was awake. How else would they have known?

The countess studied her three visitors with a blank stare. Adam, she remembered well. She seemed to dream of the man constantly. He haunted her. Lord Connor looked the same as she remembered him except his hair was a bit longer. His eyes were just as blue as always but the laughter was missing. They were cloudy with concern.

The woman, exotically beautiful and seductive even in prim brown serge and a severe hairstyle, was a complete mystery to her. She had never seen her before, of that she was sure. Any woman that beautiful would be indelibly marked in any woman's brain as the ideal one wants to be but will never achieve.

*She looks like a whore,* said a jealous little part of her brain. Bri immediately castigated herself for such an uncharitable thought. The woman was obviously there to help her get over whatever illness had confined her to her bed.

Her bed? No, it wasn't her bed, she thought, glancing around with interest. Where was she?

"Where am I?" She whispered since it was all she could do at the moment.

Adam stepped forward and locked eyes with her. "You are at Lockwood. My house in London."

The last was unnecessary. She suddenly remembered everything. The fear dogging her every footstep; the certainty that tonight was the night the master would come to take his pleasure of her; the realization that she had nowhere to go and night was falling; the intense hunger pangs that resulted in months of stealing to avoid starvation; her eventual capture and arrest; the cold stone of Newgate Prison; and the acceptance that she was going to die.

But she didn't die. Adam rescued her.

Only to turn her over to the very ones who intended her harm.

She knew she should be grateful to Adam Prestwich for saving her from hanging but she couldn't get past the fact that he was part of the reason she had ended up there in the first place. If he hadn't been tracking her so assiduously for over a year, she could have stayed in the last tolerable position she'd held. She could have stayed with Verena, Lord Connor's wife. They were friends. Bri badly needed a friend.

She felt so betrayed, by Adam, by her family, by everyone and anyone who should mean something to her. It was a depressing thought.

She realized Lord Connor was speaking.

"I'm sorry. What?"

He smiled and placed the back of his hand on her forehead. The fever had definitely broken. He was relieved. It had been fully five days since he had introduced Miss Emerson to her duties until this exact moment occurred. He had begun to wonder himself if she would recover.

"I merely said that your fever has broken and you should be right as a trivet in no time," he replied cheerfully. "The only challenge now is to get you back to a healthy weight."

"I will take care of that, my lord."

Adam bestowed a warm smile on Raven. She had been a godsend for the past five days. After telling the manager at the theater that she needed a vacation, Raven had actually moved in. She had not been from Bri's bedside for longer than a few moments at a time. She even slept on a cot by the bed at night.

He had been tempted to coax her into his bed at least one of those nights but even he knew better than to offend his servants in such a way.

Bri caught the look that Adam sent the mystery woman and she felt a fierce urge to slap her face. Her feeling of pique was suspiciously like jealousy. But that was impossible! That would suggest that she wanted Adam Prestwich for herself. And she most certainly did not!

The woman turned to her then and smiled with genuine friendliness and an awareness of something in her dark eyes that the countess couldn't even begin to understand. Lord Connor took the woman's hand and dropped a light kiss on her cheek before taking his leave. Adam followed him out, leaving Bri alone with the stranger.

"Who are you?"

Raven smiled again. "I am Raven Emerson." She dipped the most graceful curtsy Bri had ever seen.

"Why do you curtsy?" Bri asked curiously. She hadn't been curtsied to in over three years. It was something she had been used to at one time, but not anymore.

"I am not exactly sure who you are—Adam has left it up to you to tell me if you so choose—but I know that you are my social superior."

"If you don't know who I am, how do you know I'm your superior?" Bri whispered with a frown. She felt a strange pang that this goddess referred to Adam by his given name.

"I am nothing but an actress," Miss Emerson replied in her strangely husky voice. "Everyone is my superior. I am of that breed that is studiously ignored by the ladies and secretly loved by the gentlemen." She laughed lightly.

"You're a wh—" She couldn't bring herself to finish the word. Which was very strange considering the less than ladylike way she had spoken to Adam less than a week ago.

"A whore? Yes, I am. It is a fact I must contend with for the present."

There was a thread of self-loathing in her voice that Bri could understand very well. Circumstances and desperation had caused her to make some decisions of which she was not proud. But she was raised to believe that a young lady does not do certain things. What was this actress taught that made her unaccepting of her role in life?

"You need to rest."

Adam stood in the doorway, leaning against the frame. A lock of black hair lay across his brow just begging to be brushed away. He had a look of relief and amusement on his handsome face but his eyes were concerned. She realized the concern was all for her and felt a warm glow deep inside. She smiled at him.

"I'm a little hungry, actually."

Raven glanced at Adam and he gave an almost imperceptible nod. The actress disappeared through the doorway.

Adam sauntered into the room and sat on the bed, facing Bri. "Does she know who you are?"

"No."

"Did she tell you who she is?"

"She did. And her tone said far more than her words." There was censure in her tone. "Why do you keep her as your mistress when she clearly does not want to sell her body?"

Unsure how to respond to this revelation, he retorted lamely, "She is an actress."

The countess cocked one delicately arched brow at him. "Indeed?" was all she said.

He refused to be drawn. He could tell she was very quickly regaining her fighting spirit and he had no desire to be her first victim.

"How are you feeling?" he asked instead.

"I feel tired, hungry, and restless. I'm bored, Mr. Prestwich. And I like Miss Emerson. Or is it Mrs. Emerson? It doesn't matter. I don't care if she pleasures every man she comes across. I like her."

He was absurdly glad that Bri liked Raven. It made no sense. "Good, because you will be spending the next few weeks with Raven at your beck and call. And it's *Miss* Emerson."

"Why have you hired an actress as my nurse?"

"Truthfully, I didn't," he answered. "Con did so against my better judgment and she accepted."

Bri gave him a speaking glance. "You were reluctant to bring her here. Why? Were you worried over my sensibilities? I am speechless with shock."

"Doubtful," Adam muttered sarcastically. He studied her for a moment while she fidgeted with the coverlet.

"So," Bri finally said more to end the silence than in any true desire to know, "why has she agreed to play the part of my nurse?"

"She is doing more than playing a part. She has experience nursing the sick. And for the time being, we are keeping your presence a secret," he added reluctantly.

"You haven't contacted my family?" Her tone was frankly incredulous.

"No. I felt it would be best to make sure you are healthy before I take you there."

Bri closed her eyes and sighed. "And to think I had believed you almost human."

He stiffened. "Excuse me?"

"You're still taking me back. Do you have any idea to what you are turning me over?"

He relaxed. "Tell me," he requested gently.

"Maybe later," she replied without opening her eyes.

Raven entered the room then. She smiled at Adam and said, teasingly, "Would you like to do the honors, Adam?"

He grimaced. "No, thank you, my dear. I will leave the nursing to the professionals." He stood and moved towards the door.

As he passed Raven, she whispered, "I thought you were doing quite well, sir. She loves you, you know."

That stopped him. "She...*what*?" He turned hard pale eyes on her.

Raven smiled at him, her black eyes twinkling with secret mirth. "And you are in love with her."

Connor checked his patient for the last time the following day. He pronounced her to be well on the road to recovery. Provided she continued to hold down the little that she managed to eat, she would be fit as a fiddle in no time at all. Then he had smiled, kissed her affectionately on the cheek, wished her well, and took his leave.

Adam had watched the whole impassively until his friend had leaned down to kiss her cheek. He knew it was the most innocent gesture imaginable since Connor loved his wife and was completely faithful to her. But Adam could not stop the stab of unreasoning jealousy that caused thoughts of cheerfully strangling his best friend to leap into his mind.

He squashed the urge and was able to bid the other man a civil goodbye. Connor seemed to think something in his salutation was quite funny. He was still laughing as he mounted his horse and rode away.

Raven was still in residence, of course, but Adam had successfully avoided her since she had voiced her henwitted opinion on something about which she knew absolutely nothing.

He most certainly did not love the Countess of Rothsmere!

He found her to be irritating, headstrong, willful, and a royal pain. He was NOT in love with her.

And she wasn't even pretty, he thought maliciously in an attempt to dissolve the image of her he had stored in the back of his mind when searching for her. She was too thin, and too wispy, and too pale, and her hair too dull to be pretty. He diligently ignored the voice of logic in his head reminding him that up until about a week ago she had been starving to death.

Raven noticed the intense look in Adam's eyes and asked Mrs. Campion to help her with something. The two women exited the room, leaving Adam alone with Bri.

"That was very elegantly done, was it not?"

There was a smile in the countess's voice as she said this and Adam found he had to suppress an answering grin.

"Whatever do you mean?" he asked benignly.

Bri just smiled at him. "What would you like to know first, my dear Mr. Prestwich?" she asked. "It would be a shame to waste this opportunity for you to pick my brain."

Adam sat in the hard chair by the bed—and wondered why he hadn't had the blasted thing replaced with something more comfortable. He shook away the thought and concentrated on his unwilling guest.

"So talk," he commanded curtly after a few moments of tense silence on his part and amused silence on hers.

"So talk?" she repeated, drawing out the two words in a horrible drawl worthy of Brummell himself. "I am suddenly very fatigued," she said softly as she lay back on the pillows and feigned weariness. She peeked at him through half-lowered lids and was amused to see his annoyance writ plain on his attractive face.

Attractive? Where had that traitorous thought come from?

"Cut line, brat," Adam retorted rudely. "Tell me what the devil possessed you to run away from the safety and protection of your family with nothing more than the clothes on your back."

Bri stared at him with something akin to contempt. Her emerald eyes flashed with dislike, anger, and…fear? No, not fear. Adam refused to believe Bri would fear anything. She was too intrepid, too brave, too stubborn and too damned…well, mean, for lack of a better word, to be afraid of anything.

And yet, just days ago she had admitted that she was scared.

Adam pushed this uncomfortable thought aside and concentrated on getting Lady Rothsmere to talk.

"Do you really want to know, Adam?" she asked scathingly. "Do you want to hear the story in its entirety? Or do you want to hear that I was just bored and looking for a lark which, unfortunately, when found went horribly wrong? Do you want the truth or what you believe to be true?"

He felt an unaccountable urge to fidget at the words that were almost exactly the same as he had uttered to Connor at White's recently.

He noticed her hands were clenched painfully tight in her lap, the knuckles white. Her eyes were as hard as the jewels they so closely resembled. He was right, she wasn't scared. She was angry. Then he saw her lower lip tremble pathetically and wondered if she would use tears to manipulate him as all women did.

Bri didn't give in to the tears that threatened. She would die before she'd cry in front of this man. But she wanted to make him feel remorse for the thinly veiled insult on her intelligence.

Lifting her chin a notch, Bri met Adam's gray-green eyes and said vehemently, but quietly, "I ran away, Mr. Prestwich, because I wasn't ready to die!"

# Chapter Eight

"What?"

"Did I stutter?" Bri sneered. "Do you not understand the King's English? I didn't want to die. It is a reasonable thing to wish for when you haven't even reach your eighteenth year."

"You exaggerate, my lady, surely. Who would want you dead?"

His tone was as disbelieving as could be although his face was carefully blank. He may as well call her a liar to her face and end their conversation. She could tell he wouldn't believe a word she had to say.

"Talking to you is pointless, Adam," she replied wearily, suddenly tired of fighting with him or trying to get him to understand. "You won't believe a word I tell you if you even listen at all."

Adam regretted making his disbelief so obvious. He strove for a conciliatory tone when he said gently, "I apologize, Bri, if I seemed less than believing. But if you think about it, it does seem a trifle farfetched. One of the leading families in England tries to kill off their heiress? In the hopes of getting her title and inheritance, I assume. It is your family you are accusing, is it not?"

She nodded and watched him closely. He was being very careful with his expression, she noted. He revealed nothing more than polite interest. Except his eyes. Bri realized with a start that Adam, for some reason, was not masking his emotions from his eyes. She saw contempt, derision, and cynicism mingling in the gray-green depths. And there, in the farthest reaches, beyond all the negative emotions, she saw concern.

It was the concern that made her talk although she wasn't foolish enough to totally discount the derogatory feelings he held in check.

Her face and voice were devoid of emotion as she spoke. Adam wondered how much of her tale was truth and how much was calculated to manipulate his nobler feelings of protectiveness and sympathy.

"I grew up knowing that I would one day inherit my father's title and vast wealth. I was the only child of my parents' union and mama died when I was five. Papa's title was one that could pass to a daughter as well as a son. He died when I was nearly seventeen and I became the Countess of Rothsmere.

"I was left in the care of my mother's brother and his wife, the Duke and Duchess of Corning, my father's sister and her husband, the Earl and Countess of Fenton, and my father's brother, the Duke of Westbury. They were all ecstatic when they discovered they had complete control over my money and me until the day I turn twenty-five. I was ordered to marry the man of their choice."

Adam smiled despite his doubt in the veracity of her story. "And you rebelled, I would guess."

"At first," she replied complacently. "Until I met him. He was everything I ever dreamed of in a husband."

Adam experienced a sick feeling in his stomach at her confession. There was a wistful note in her voice that suggested that she still had feelings for this man, whoever he was.

He opened his mouth to tell her tersely to continue but found himself saying instead, "Who was he?"

Bri turned her head and regarded Adam in surprise. If she didn't know better, she would have thought he sounded jealous. She smiled slowly. "It doesn't matter. It didn't work out."

Prestwich grunted and told her gruffly to continue her tale. She stifled a smirk and complied.

"Things did not work out as I wanted. I thought myself in love with the gentleman chosen for me. Until I overheard a conversation between him and Corning. Once my betrothed was my husband and gained control of my money, he was to give half to the duke and certain secrets about the gentleman, and I use the term loosely, would not be revealed to the *ton*. After the marriage was consummated, he could go his own way.

"I decided he could go his own way a bit earlier than expected. I marched right into the room and announced to the men attempting to ruin my life that I would die rather than marry the bastard." She suddenly laughed. Her eyes twinkled merrily as she regarded Adam. "I used that word when I confronted them, Adam. I didn't know that *that* was the big secret."

Adam stared at her in shock then smiled, as her laughter was infectious. He could imagine what sort of commotion ensued after such a declaration.

He realized he was being manipulated into relaxing his guard against her feminine wiles and he resolutely hardened his heart. His smile was replaced with a frown and he ordered her to continue.

The smile in her eyes died and the smile on her face turned cynical and mocking. "Don't let my obvious enjoyment of the situation color your views, my dear sir. I would hate for you to be disappointed lest I confirm your idea that women are the very devil."

"So you ran away to avoid marriage to a man obviously not worthy of you and decided that whoring on the streets was infinitely better?" His own voice was mocking and he watched her closely.

"I would have been much better off as some man's whore than that man's wife, I do assure you. At least a whore has the right to leave should she wish. A wife is little better than a slave to her husband's whims and freakish starts," she retorted bitterly. Her tone softened only slightly as she continued. "But no, I did not run away for that reason. I did and still do feel that anything is better than spending my life with a man who has betrayed me. But the real reason I ran away was the ultimatum put upon me. I was to marry Lord—" She glanced at him sharply. His eyes were narrowed suspiciously. She had almost let the name slip. "Let's call him Lord Nobody, shall we?"

"Lord Nobody? Very clever, I must say," Adam responded dryly.

"Is everything all right?" Raven poked her head into the room, her dark eyes bright with curiosity. "Have you need of anything?"

"A straitjacket, perhaps?" Adam said beneath his breath. He smiled at his mistress. "No, Raven, we're fine. But have a tea tray sent up in about an hour."

Raven threw a worried look at Bri, nodded and left.

When Adam returned his attention to his guest, he noticed her face was drained of color and she was trembling. Her hands were wreaking havoc with the counterpane and she seemed to be staring at nothing. What the devil was wrong? He was out of his chair and beside her on the bed within two heartbeats. He reached out to touch her and she flinched away from him.

"That was not amusing," she whispered.

Adam sat on the bed beside her, nonplussed by her comment. "What wasn't amusing?"

"Straitjackets are horrible things. I couldn't move and I couldn't get away. It was horrible."

Adam took her by the shoulders and turned her towards him. The thought in his mind was too terrible to contemplate. Her eyes held more than just the horror of being alone and wondering where the next meal would come from and when. She looked lost in a memory too traumatic for words. She reminded him very much of Verena Northwicke when that young matron had told him of her rape. He shuddered.

"Bri, what are you saying?" She remained silent. He shook her a little. "Tell me!"

She met his gaze unblinkingly and loosened her clenched hands to grip the lapels of his riding coat.

"Oh my God," Adam breathed. "They locked you in a madhouse." He saw the truth in her eyes and he drew her against his chest, rubbing her back soothingly. He felt her start to shake then her arms went around his waist and she held him so tight he found it difficult to draw a deep breath.

He didn't want to believe it was her family that had done such a hateful thing. He was unsure exactly who *they* were, but someone had done a terrible disservice to this vibrant, lively girl. They had destroyed her innocence and taken away every dream a young girl has about her life and the love she will one day find.

She was crying. Not wrenching sobs, but quiet weeping that cut right to his heart. She was genuinely distressed. It wasn't a ploy to gain his sympathy or sway his decision. It was fear and terror.

"Bri, you're okay now, love. Don't cry, please."

With the tears finally abating and the fear receding, Bri was able to regain control of her rioting emotions. She was disgusted with herself for losing control but she hadn't thought of that time in the madhouse for so very long. She'd had no idea the mere thought would freeze her back in time.

She pulled out of Adam's arms and only then realized when she looked into his worried countenance that he had been very comforting and tender. Her heart gave a little leap in her breast.

She took a deep breath. "I apologize for that unseemly display, Adam. It was unlike me."

"Yes, it was," he replied thoughtfully, making no move to leave her side. He found the bed a good sight more comfortable than the hell-chair and decided he wasn't moving unless she actually asked him to do so.

He wasn't going to move, she thought. She wanted him to move. She didn't like his concern. It made her think things she had no business thinking about. Like how good it felt to be held by him. And what it would feel like to have his lips pressed to hers. Her body responded to the thought and she cursed it roundly for being such a traitor. Adam Prestwich was the enemy.

She wanted to tell him to move. She wanted to tell him to get out. Of her life, preferably. But there was really nothing she could do. If he wanted to sit on the bed, so be it.

"Now, where was I?"

"You were supposed to marry Lord, uh, *Nobody*, I believe," Adam supplied helpfully. He turned so he was facing her, crossed his arms over his chest and prepared to be amazed at her powers of invention.

She smiled faintly. "Lord Nobody, yes. Well, I couldn't do that. I told them I wouldn't do that. Corning held a counsel of war with the rest of the family. They told me it was Lord...Nobody or he would put me, he would...he would send me away." She looked down at her tightly clasped hands, unable to meet his eyes.

"Put you...where?" Adam asked.

"Exactly where he did put me, in a madhouse."

Her voice was blank, her face was blank, but that haunted look was dawning in her wide eyes again. "No, love. Stay here with me. What happened next?"

It was the endearment that snapped her out of it. Her eyes narrowed as he watched her. "My cousin succeeding in freeing me. Then he had to leave and I was again on my own. So I ran away and here we are," she ended on a derogatory note.

"Yes, here we are. And you spent the intervening time working where you could and doing what you had to in order to survive, correct?"

She eyed him suspiciously. "Yes, why?"

Adam smiled blandly. "Just trying to reconcile a few things in my own mind, that's all."

"Why don't you just ask me if I was whoring on the streets to keep from starving?" she snapped angrily.

His curiosity got the better of him. "Why did you not just set yourself up as some man's mistress? You have the beauty and the spirit to be a first-class courtesan."

"Thank you for that assessment of my character, Mr. High and Mighty. I didn't take a protector because I couldn't stand the thought of what I'd have to do with the bloody bastard. Men are all disgusting pigs."

Adam peered closely at her, moving his head from side to side as if looking for something. His intense look was making Bri decidedly nervous.

"What?'

"I am sure there is a lady in there somewhere," Adam responded with a thoughtful frown. He shook his head sadly. "No, perhaps not. She must have died some time ago, I should imagine."

"She did," Bri retorted dryly. "I killed her."

Adam had to smile at that. She certainly was an interesting young lady.

He sought to bring their discussion back to the subject they needed to explore. "If you couldn't stand the duties of a mistress, how did you, to use your own words, sell yourself on the streets?"

"I didn't. I've been raped several times but I have never consented to having relations with any man." Her voice was dead and her eyes were closed as she said this.

He was amazed at her calm tone. He felt his own heart stop and then speed up alarmingly. He wanted to destroy every bastard who ever touched her. He was disgusted by his own intense feelings and further disgusted by his readiness to believe her protestations.

He stood and bowed. He had to get away from her before she managed to make him believe the whole sordid tale. "I have some business to attend to this afternoon, my lady. I will leave you in Raven's capable hands."

# Chapter Nine

"What was that all about?" Raven asked as she directed the maid with the tea tray.

Bri shrugged but said nothing.

"Very well," Raven replied equably. "Would you like tea, my dear?"

"I think I would like to rest," Bri answered wearily.

She did sound tired, Raven thought compassionately. She wondered what Adam had been thinking to tax her about her past at such a time. Raven would swear that sometimes the man was completely oblivious.

"Would you like to eat something first? You really must if you are to regain your strength."

"Oh, very well," Bri replied ungraciously. "Just so you leave me alone."

Raven complacently placed a tray over the young lady's lap and handed her a spoon. "Do you think you can manage on your own?" she asked with quiet concern.

"What the devil is this rot?" Bri exclaimed as she examined the bowl before her, ignoring Raven's inquiry.

"That rot, as you so quaintly put it, is cook's never-fail remedy for ailing strength. She says you are to drink every last drop or you'll have her to contend with." Raven smiled brilliantly. "And I reckon Adam will be back in here to put a bug in your ear as well."

"Let him, I'm not eating that slop," Bri responded querulously.

"If you don't get your strength back," the actress retorted slyly, "then how do you suppose you will be able to escape Adam again?"

Bri shot her a penetrating look. Then she grinned. "You're right, you know. I wouldn't want him to get lazy and fat just because I neglected to give him a run for his money."

"That's the spirit! Now eat it all. Can you manage?" she asked again.

"Yes, you can go beard the lion in his den as I know you are itching to do," Bri replied with a smile.

Raven smiled back and that was the start of a most unconventional friendship between a titled lady of good birth and upbringing and a confessed lady of the night.

Adam was in his study going over his accounts when Raven entered the room. Her wool skirts swirled around her and he wondered why she still insisted on wearing her "governess" costumes when everyone knew who she was and what she was to him.

"To what do I owe this unexpected pleasure?" Adam asked politely as he rose from his chair.

"I'm curious," his mistress commented as she came around to his side of the desk and put her arms around his waist. She looked up at him with a benign expression on her beautiful face. "Do you want her dead or do you just delight in tormenting her?"

Adam placed his hands on Raven's shoulders. His voice was calmly inquiring when he replied but his eyes held dangerous sparks. "What business is that of yours, my dear?"

"I like her, Adam. I won't let you destroy her."

"As I've destroyed you?" he asked quietly.

Raven felt a lump in her throat. Did she secretly blame Adam for her own lack of moral conviction? She supposed she did, somewhat. But how on earth would he guess such a thing?

Adam tensed his hands on her shoulders. Her black eyes met his with a look of such bewildered sadness that he was taken aback.

"You do believe that. You think I destroyed you." It was not a question. Adam felt hurt that she would blame him. If she had simply said something, he never would have taken her on.

"Please don't change the subject," she said in an attempt to draw his attention away from her. "I want to know what you plan to do with that poor girl."

"And I want to know why you accepted my offer of protection when it wasn't what you wanted," he countered softly. His eyes held an implacable look of determination. "Who do you think is going to get their way?"

Raven found herself weakening under the onslaught of tenderness she saw in his eyes. She was not naïve enough to believe he was in love with her. She knew it was nothing more than a pleasurable arrangement for him to keep her. She even knew he liked her most of the time. But she never considered he might actually care for her as anything more than a release for pent-up emotions.

Raven squeezed her eyes tightly shut against the tears that threatened.

Adam regarded his mistress steadily. He reached out and wiped away a tear that escaped her tightly closed eyes. He wondered if she was in love with him.

He knew he wasn't in love with her. He realized his world would be just as painful and barely tolerable with or without her in it. But he did care about her. He imagined love went much deeper than mere caring.

If she were to tell him right this moment that she had found somebody new, he would let her go with nothing more than a thought as to if the man would treat her as she deserved. If so, he would be happy to let her go. It was a strange realization to have about the woman one was holding so closely in one's arms at the very moment the thought occurred.

Her eyes opened and her pain was visible and deeply touching. Why had he ever agreed to take her on? he wondered again. He had known beforehand that she was innocent. All he'd had to do was tell her he had no dealings with virgins.

*You didn't believe her,* a voice taunted him.

Of course, he hadn't believed her. She was a woman, after all. All women lied to achieve their goals. Look at Lady Rothsmere. She was a prime example of scheming womankind. And he didn't believe a word she said about her family.

Or so he told himself.

"Do you love me?" he asked abruptly.

Raven started. "Do I love you?" she repeated numbly, her emotions still whirling from his unusual kiss. "I suppose I do, in a way. Why?"

"I don't know," Adam replied thoughtfully. "It just seemed important to ask, that's all."

Raven laid her head on his shoulder. His hand came up to rest on the back of her neck and just stayed there, his thumb stroking the side of her neck in a comforting pattern. They stood like that for a while before Raven sighed and stepped away from him.

"I am very disappointed in myself," she told him tartly. "I

came here to beard the lion in his den and then allowed said lion to distract me from my task. Shame on me." She smiled.

Adam steered her to a chair and then sat down himself. "Beard away," he replied with a little less than his usual cynicism.

"What are your plans for Miss Bri?"

"Miss Bri? Has she still not told you who she is, then?"

"No she has not. But I think she will, given time."

"What makes you think that?" he asked, truly perplexed.

Raven favored him with an amused, mysterious grin. "Just a feeling I have."

Adam quirked an eyebrow at her and his lips curled into a half-smile. "Indeed?"

"Indeed," she replied confidently. "I have a feeling we are bound to be friends."

Adam's smile disappeared. "No, you're not."

"I hardly think you have any right to decide my friends, Adam."

"But I do have a right to decide who may or may not associate with my guest." He sighed and shoved a hand through his dark locks. "Damn it, I knew it was a bad idea to bring you here," he muttered half to himself.

Raven controlled her temper. She had to know what Adam planned to do with Bri. "All of that aside," she replied in a tone that suggested they would argue about her choice in friends later, "what do you plan to do with her?"

Adam looked at her and for the first time felt like throwing her out on her ear. He had never found her particularly annoying before but now he felt like giving the woman her *congé*. Blast, women were the devil! What would she do if he told her that Bri must go back?

He couldn't take any chances in losing the chit again. "I will tell you when I've reached a decision," he replied evasively.

Raven could tell that was the only answer she was going to receive at that moment. "Fine," she capitulated. She had some doubts that he would tell her, but there was nothing else she could do for the time being. "But as her nurse, I must ask you to please refrain from tiring her out as you did today."

Lady Rothsmere plucked nervously at the coverlet on the bed. She eyed her companion with some misgiving.

She didn't know why she was so uncertain about asking this particular woman questions. She had, after all, spent the past week doing little more than converse with her and laugh with her and become closer and closer. So why did she feel so reluctant to ask her what she really wanted to know?

Probably because it would be rude, vulgar, and impertinent for her to do so. Bri had never let such things stop her before. Those very reasons had often spurred her on to somewhat reckless acts, as a matter of fact.

But now she found herself facing an actress from Drury Lane, someone undeserving of a countess's notice let alone her friendship for the simple reason that she had chosen acting as her means of survival. However, Bri couldn't get around the feeling that it would be beyond rude to ask Raven what she wanted to know.

And why did she even care? It wasn't as if she was interested in Adam herself. The man was infuriating and rude and stubborn and hardheaded and cynical and...and...

Bri realized she had just described herself.

This realization stilled her hands ensuring the coverlet's survival. Were they really so much alike? It wasn't possible. If she were like him...the thought did not deserve the attention she was giving it. And neither did he.

"It might relieve your mind if you just ask me whatever it is you want to know."

Looking up, Bri encountered amused black eyes. She smiled slightly and looked away. Raven continued to look at her expectantly.

"Do you love him?" Bri blurted out before the thought had even formed in her head.

Raven's perfectly arched brows quirked upward. "I assume you are referring to Adam," she replied in her slightly husky voice. Her gaze turned enigmatic, mysterious, as if she knew a secret of great import and she was debating whether or not to share. "I also assume you have a good reason for asking, so I will tell you. In a way, of course I do. He is a very dear friend after all and has played a big part in my survival." She smiled. "No, I am not in love with him."

Bri released the breath she hadn't been aware she was even holding. "I am completely disgusted with myself," she said heatedly. "And Adam. I am beyond well, yet here I sit, in bed, as if

I am still ill. Why can't I walk about? I would like to go outside. I would like to feel less like an invalid and more like a human being."

Miss Emerson chuckled. "That explains your disgust for Adam. What about you?"

Bri flushed, embarrassed for the first time for her impertinence. "I had no business asking you such a personal question, especially considering your relationship with Adam, and I am severely disappointed in myself for succumbing to temptation."

"I see."

"I'm sorry."

"Don't be. I don't mind. But I wouldn't go asking Adam the same question," she warned lightly. "He may lie or stretch the truth a bit just to try to set you off. You know how he is."

Adam entered the room at that moment and both women wondered how much he had heard, if anything. His look gave nothing away since it was a well-bred blank and his eyes were shuttered.

"Good afternoon, ladies," he said with a slightly mocking bow that indicated his belief that there were no such creatures present in that particular room. "I trust I find you both well."

"Yes. Why the devil am I still confined to this bloody bed?"

One black brow rose imperiously. Adam stared at Bri until she flushed with embarrassment for the second time that day. She cursed him in her head and corrected, "I am well, thank you, Mr. Prestwich. I hope you are well?" Her tone implied she wished no such thing. "Will I be able to leave my bed soon?"

Adam let his amusement show. His lips quirked upward and he crossed his arms over his chest. "Why haven't you defied me?" he asked in a most conversational tone.

Bri was determined not to let him goad her. She smiled brilliantly. "I would never do anything so vulgar as defy my temporary guardian," she replied with a sweetness that was truly awful to behold. "Why, what would he think of me were I to do such a hoydenish thing?"

"He would probably think you were actually better," Prestwich retorted dryly. "How can I be sure you are strong enough to go home if you are still not acting like the Bri I know?"

# Chapter Ten

"Oh, dear God, you're sending me back," Bri breathed in sudden trepidation.

She was surprised that she had actually believed that he would see the truth in her story and not take her back. Had she really wanted to make a knight-errant out of the infamous Mr. Adam Prestwich? Everyone knew what a cold-hearted devil he was. *She* knew personally what a cold-hearted devil he was. Why would he change for her?

"Adam, you can't possibly send her back there. Do you—"

"Leave us, Raven," Prestwich commanded curtly. "This doesn't concern you."

He advanced into the room. Raven stood her ground and glared up at him defiantly. "I will not let you do it, Adam."

Adam's hand shot out and clamped painfully on her wrist. "You will obey me in this, woman," he bit out as he propelled her to the door. He shoved her through, closed the door, and locked it.

"That was a trifle harsh, don't you think?"

Adam approached the bed. He stood next to it, his arms once again crossed over his broad chest. "Perhaps," he admitted. "But I find I have no patience for females at the moment."

"That is hardly an acceptable excuse for manhandling a weaker creature than you, Mr. Prestwich."

A grunt was the only indication he even heard her words. "You are going home today, Lady Rothsmere. Prepare yourself for it."

Bri sighed. She was suddenly so tired. Tired of running. Tired of fighting. Tired of…life.

"Fine," she replied woodenly.

Adam noticed her change in mood and wondered at it. He suspected that she was merely trying to trick him into letting down his guard so she could escape again.

"Are you going to try to escape?" he finally asked after studying her for several tense moments on his part.

"No."

"Do I have your word?"

She hesitated. "Yes. You have my word I will not attempt to escape," she replied solemnly.

"Thank you."

Adam turned to leave. Bri felt all her old anger return for a moment and she glared at his retreating back wishing she had a knife to stick there. She settled for words.

"You're an unconscionable bastard, Adam Prestwich. I feel sorry for your wife."

Adam froze. How did she…? No, it wasn't possible. He turned around slowly, fixing her with a basilisk stare. "What did you say?"

Bri returned his gaze with one of her own. "You will marry one day and I pity the poor girl who is forced to accept your hand."

Adam's relief was so great, he actually smiled, albeit mockingly. "Well, I will never marry, so you need not trouble your *kind heart* with her miserable fortune."

It was every bit as bad as she had thought it would be. She stood in the rigidly formal drawing room of the Duke of Corning's London residence in Grosvenor Square. Well, it was actually one of *her* homes but this point was moot at the moment. Adam had retreated a pace but he was still within reach and her family virtually surrounded them.

They were all there: both dukes and their wives, the earl and countess, and even her cousin Viscount Breckon. It crossed her mind that Levi was missing and she felt like she was completely friendless. He was the only one she could count on to take her side.

Her blasted family fawned over her for quite half-an-hour exclaiming over how worried they were and how naughty she was. It was all just a show for Adam, she knew, and he just stood there like a big dumb animal and said nothing unless asked a direct question.

Bri watched her nemesis surreptitiously while her Aunt Clara lamented the loss of her dark red locks. Honestly, Bri didn't really miss them. Her hair had been thick and heavy causing her constant headaches. Since her convalesce at Lockwood, her hair had grown to a more manageable length and recovered its deep red luster. It now closely resembled a fashionable crop.

Adam met her gaze suddenly and she realized the mocking look had gone to be replaced by an unreadable emotion. Puzzled, she looked back at Aunt Clara, Countess of Fenton.

Aunt Clara was a short, flighty little thing with more hair than wit. She adopted the mannerisms of a débutante although she was well into her fiftieth year. When presented to Adam she had simpered and flirted awfully. Bri was impressed with his ability to hide the disgust he had to feel.

"My dear girl, you have lost weight as well, have you not? This is just dreadful! However shall you find a husband looking the way you do?" Aunt Clara twisted her hands together in distress.

"Don't be a twit, Clara," the Duchess of Corning inserted sharply. "She doesn't need looks. She has money and a title. Besides, her betrothed is awaiting her."

"What?" Adam and Bri exclaimed simultaneously. They exchanged looks of consternation although Adam's stance had not changed. He still stood a little from her with his left hand fingering his quizzing glass and his right hand shoved in the pocket of his pantaloons. Surprise had him momentarily stiffening and the hand on his glass paused for a fraction of a second. But then he was in complete control again.

Lady Corning turned a haughty look on Mr. Prestwich. "You may go now, sir. You have completed your task, I think." Her nose rose another notch, if that was even possible.

Adam restrained his sudden urge to toss the old bat out the window and bowed instead. He threw a look at Bri and took his leave.

Bri watched him go and wondered why she felt even more friendless than she had before. Then she faced her family and shivered. Corning was wearing a smirk and his wife was staring at her disdainfully. Aunt Clara was still fidgeting, as usual, and the Duke of Westbury was looking mighty pleased with himself. The viscount stood by the window, looking out on the square as if the drawing room proceedings held no interest for him. The Earl of Fenton's expression was impassive and she wondered if perhaps he had succumbed to his past habit of taking laudanum on a regular basis. His eyes looked decidedly glassy.

It took all of her willpower not to dash after Adam and beg him to take her away. She knew that the dukes' plans had changed and she knew they would be even worse than before.

He stopped just outside the front door and looked up. He caught the look of cunning on Viscount Breckon's face. He had to repress a shiver.

Adam shook his head and vaulted into his phaeton. His tiger handed him the reins and Adam set off, barely giving the lad time to leap on the back.

Adam drove through the late morning streets of London at a reckless pace, trying to outrun his conscience. He shouldn't have left her there with those people. But what could he have possibly done? She was underage. They had control. Her family contained two dukes, an earl, a viscount, and a few minor titles as well. Adam Prestwich, baronet, quite simply lacked the power to help her.

He had the money, of that he was sure. Westbury had barely a feather to fly with; Corning had not much more than that. Of the viscount Adam knew little, but he suspected that he was a trifle lean in the pocket as well. Everyone knew that Fenton spent every cent he had on his drug habit so Adam knew there was no money there. There was a baron in there somewhere but Adam didn't even know his name much less his financial situation.

But did she really need the help? Or was her family telling the truth when they told him she was just being a spoiled brat? What on earth had possessed the Earl of Rothsmere to leave her in the care of impecunious relatives?

A vision of haunted emerald eyes flashed before his eyes and he jerked the reins. It took him a few moments to bring his team back under control while Jem muttered something about ham-fisted driving.

Why did he have to remember that now? She would have to be a better actress than Raven to have been lying when she told him about the straitjacket. She had cried. Piteously. It was very unlike Bri to cry.

Especially in front of him.

Adam drew to a halt before his mansion but didn't move to step down. Jem ran around to the horses' heads and waited patiently.

Adam wished Connor was still in Town. He might have some idea of how to help.

Damn it, she didn't need his help! He had *helped* enough. But he had to do something.

"Get back on or get out of the way," Adam commanded curtly, coming to a sudden decision. Jem jumped back on and they were off again, this time to Haymarket.

"You want me to *what*?" asked Raven in disbelief.

"Don't sound as though I'm asking you to commit some crime. I just want to know what Breckon is up to. How would you do that without putting out a few lures?"

Adam's tone matched his expression of unconcern. He leaned back in his chair, regarding his mistress complacently, waiting for her response.

"No, Adam. In fact, I am surprised you even have the audacity to ask me to do anything for you."

His black brows lifted slightly at this. "Why?"

Raven stared at him for several shocked moments. He was truly perplexed that she would be upset. Angrily, she shoved her hand under his nose and snapped, "Look at that and try to tell me I have no right to be upset with you!"

On her wrist was a dark bruise about an inch wide. Adam looked from her wrist to her dark, flashing eyes. His expression changed not a jot as he said, "I apologize."

Whether he was apologizing for inflicting the bruise or for assuming she would help under such circumstances was a mystery to Raven. She did know, however, that it was the best she could expect from her protector, so she shook her head in exasperation and returned to their former topic.

"I would rather not hint to the viscount that I have any interest in him. He is a snake and a personal crony of Percival Winters. No two more dangerous men do I know." A thoughtful expression crossed her beautiful features. "Except perhaps the Duke of Derringer. But even with his ruthless reputation, he still possesses something human."

Adam's curiosity was piqued by his companion's assessment of a man society deemed the most dangerous man in England, possibly the world. But he pushed it to the back of his mind and asked instead, "Are you sure about Breckon's association with Winters?"

"I am an actress, Adam. I am inundated with importuning gentleman on a regular basis. Those two are as close as inkleweavers."

Her protector pondered this a moment, then, "Forget about attracting him, then. Just watch." He rose to his feet. "And watch Bri as well. Inform me the instant something strange occurs."

As it turned out, all their plans were for naught.

# Chapter Eleven

Lady Brianna, Countess of Rothsmere was taken from Town the day after her return to the bosom of her family. Everyone assumed she was taken home to her estate in Lancashire. But Lady Rothsmere's holdings were nearly as vast as Denbigh's, so she could be anywhere in England.

Raven watched her protector pace around her small sitting room and wondered what he could possibly do now that the object of his distress was gone.

Adam was wondering the same thing. He suspected he wouldn't see Bri again until the Season, which was still several months away. It was frustrating to realize that there was nothing he could do.

Why did he feel the need to *do* anything?

Adam stopped suddenly and stared at his mistress. She was standing off to one side of the room watching him intently. Her dark eyes were alight with worry and her mouth was set in a grim line. She wore a gown of pale blue that curved low over her perfect breasts and flowed out from the high waist in gentle folds of shimmery silk and gauze. Her hair was unbound as was her preference and lay in a sheet of shining black silk down her back. Her eyes widened as he watched her and her facial features relaxed slightly.

What the devil was he thinking? Here he was, one of the richest men in England, possessed of the most sought-after, most beautiful mistress in the realm, and he was worrying about a sharp-tongued hoyden who had made her aversion for him obvious on more than one occasion.

A slow smile of wicked intent curved his lips.

Raven saw that look and knew exactly what he was thinking. He had pushed Bri from his mind and now thought of only one thing. She smiled back and decided to enjoy what time with Adam Prestwich she had remaining. She knew it would be short.

Mary Brewster was a rawboned, grim-faced woman of indeterminate years. Her bearing was that of a warden, gruff and lacking in compassion and fellow feeling. She seemed to lack a soul.

And yet, Bri found in her a most unusual friendship.

The woman was hired to guard the young countess, it was true. And she knew it would be more than her life was worth should she try to help the poor girl. But they managed to come to an understanding: Bri knew she was better off with a guard that treated her with respect and Mary was intelligent enough to know that a headstrong girl treated with respect was less likely to give one trouble.

And so the months passed with the two women engaging in conversation and Bri avoiding her family as much as possible.

Mary was efficient in her work as ladies' maid. She had a good eye for color and a satisfactory skill in arranging hair. Bri actually would have been immensely pleased with her performance had it not been for the fact that the woman was in fact her jailer. This grated on Bri, but she could do little about it.

Lady Brianna was being constrained to marry a man ten times worse than the gentleman to whom she was engaged before. Her new fiancé was Viscount Steyne.

She remembered him from when she had worked for Lord and Lady Feldspar in Hereford. Steyne was the man who had repeatedly refused to take no for an answer whenever he had pressed his unwelcome attentions on Verena, now Lady Connor Northwicke.

He was of average height with sandy brown hair and expressionless brown eyes that were so light they appeared quite colorless. He had a pleasant face that was often marred by a sneer. His heart was as black as his reputation and Bri knew her life with him was going to be hell. But she could see no way out.

He made no secret of the fact that he was after her money and he was equally vocal on what her duties as his wife would include. He had on several occasions tried to force her to commence those duties early but she had somehow managed to avoid his attempts at rape. Brewster had always managed to be there just when Bri needed her. For this, Bri was eternally indebted to the woman.

His grace of Corning had spelled out for her the consequences should she run again.

Bri had stood silently in the pale light of early morning while she was roundly chastised for her flight more than three years ago. Her uncle was cruel and merciless in his anger and Bri just waited patiently for his tirade to end. The end was not what she had expected.

The duke had walked over to the bellpull, rang for a servant and turned back to face his niece. "You will now have the rebellion beaten out of you as it should have been years ago," he said brutally.

Bri had turned paper white.

She really shouldn't be surprised, she thought numbly after the horrible beating. It shouldn't have been any different than if a stranger had beaten her on the street. It wasn't as if any of her relatives loved her. Or anyone else for that matter.

This last thought caused such a painful wrench in her heart that she gave in and indulged in a hearty bout of tears brought on by self-pity.

So, why did she not simply run away from her problems?

Bri was tired. She was tired of running, tired of fighting, and tired of trying to stop that which was essentially unstoppable. Her family wanted her money and would stop at nothing to possess it. She gave in to this thought and allowed them to bully her. She allowed them to believe she was as broken as they ever could have wished and thereby preserved at least a modicum of her sanity.

She often thought about Adam and plotted revenge on him for returning her to such a hell. But deep down she realized that he really had had no choice. He would have been brought up on charges had he tried to help her. And that she couldn't have endured. He had saved her life after all.

Saved it for what, she wondered now. Saved her so that she could give it up to a man who would have little care for her as a person? Saved her so that she could be her family's sacrificial lamb and bear the burden of her uncle's years of stupidity and blackmail? Saved her so that she could once again face the threat of institutionalization? Saved her so that she could die a more painful, prolonged death at the hands of those who hated her?

Oh, yes, he had saved her life all right.

"Do you want to talk about it?"

Bri looked up from her contemplation of the early spring

morning outside the drawing room window and met the compassionate stare of her cousin, Levi, the Earl of Greville. She hadn't seen him since he had helped her escape from the madhouse three years ago.

She wasn't sure she was seeing him now. He stood before her in all the glory of Weston's tailoring with a sad smile on his boyishly handsome face. His deep brown eyes watched her closely and his hands knotted into fists at his sides.

Bri rose slowly from her seat and waited for him to disappear before her very eyes. He was the only one that loved her, the only one she could count on. She was sure that he wasn't real. He was conjured out of her desperation for a release from her own personal hell.

She kept repeating this to herself even as he advanced into the room and reached out to her. When his fingers very lightly brushed her cheek she was suddenly struck with the urge to weep bitterly for her sorry lot in life. But pride stiffened her spine and she was determined that Greville not know how much she was suffering.

"Talk about what, pray?" she asked languidly after hugging him quickly and offering a quick smile.

"About this marriage I hear you have contracted. Why the devil are you marrying Steyne of all people?" he demanded.

She gasped before she could think. "Where did you hear that?" she asked breathlessly. The engagement had not been announced yet and wasn't supposed to be until the start of the Season when everyone would return to Town and then know of her great good fortune in bringing the illusive and dangerous Lord Steyne up to scratch.

"At the club last week when I went to London looking for you. Steyne himself was spouting off how he had managed to capture the wealthiest heiress ever to grace London. I assume it's true. Why are you doing it?"

Bri sat down carefully and arranged the skirts of her dark brown dress around her before answering. "Because I love him," she finally replied. Her voice sounded unconvincing even to herself.

His eyes narrowed. "The devil you do," he retorted after a moment. "You have no more love for that man than I do. Tell me what is going on."

Bri gave him her coldest look. "I am marrying Lord Steyne,

Levi Sterling, and you can't stop me."

The earl was taken aback by the vehemence in her tone. And her use of his second name. She only did that when she was particularly upset with him. The only thing worse was when she started addressing him as 'my lord.'

Seeking to placate the fiery beauty that was his cousin, Greville smiled his most charming smile and seated himself beside her on the settee.

And Greville's most charming smile was nothing to take lightly. He was impossibly handsome, even Bri had to admit. And yet...she thought Adam Prestwich was far more intriguing with his dark features and cynical humor.

Pushing the infuriating Mr. Prestwich determinedly from her mind, Bri continued to glare at her beloved cousin.

"Aw, come on, Bri. You now I didn't mean anything by it. If you want to marry the bas—I mean, viscount, then far be it for me to try to convince you otherwise."

Bri almost gave in to impulse and confessed to the earl how she was being forced into all of it. Then she hardened her heart and closed her mind to the possibility of escape. The die had been cast. She would marry Viscount Steyne and hand over her money along with her freedom and whatever shred of innocence she might have retained over the last three years.

She smiled brightly at Greville and ignored the warm, cozy feeling that the thought of suicide gave her.

Dinner that night was an abomination. She and Lord Greville were treated with a cold courtesy that just bordered on contempt. Bri noticed he bore it all with fortitude although she knew he must be seething with rage. He was normally very easy-going and although he tended to get involved in some rather hair-raising and often incredibly stupid stunts, he had never been known to have a temper.

But Bri had been present when Greville had laid into her first fiancé for his ungentlemanly conduct and for that lord's part in her incarceration for her supposed madness. She was surprised the man had lived through it. Greville was a very muscular young man, larger than Adam even, who was no lightweight. Even at the age of only twenty, he had been larger than most men. And now, at age twenty-four, he was positively massive. But her intended husband had walked away with his life. Greville had merely rearranged his face until it was no longer the pretty mask it once was.

Bri had to admit to a certain amount of satisfaction at the result of the lord's pummeling. There had been enough hurt in her to want the young man to pay for his treatment of her. Now, she just felt like three years of her life had been wasted in heartache and constant fear. She would have been better off with a wastrel than the scoundrel she was now being forced to marry.

"And so we will be leaving for London for the Season," Aunt Clara said with a flutter of her bony hands.

"What?" Bri asked faintly. She had not thought she would have to endure the eyes of Society ever again. She wasn't sure she could continue her act under the watchful eyes of Adam Prestwich. Or Verena. Oh, dear, Verena would know instantly that Bri was less than pleased with her situation.

The Duke of Westbury eyed her coldly. "London, miss. Cannot you hear?" Westbury adamantly refused to address her by her title.

"I heard," Bri replied shortly. "I simply wonder at the necessity of such a step."

"Why does anyone attend the Season, think you? To see and be seen, of course," her grace of Corning said haughtily. "To grace the metropolis with our august presence."

"Dear me," Bri muttered sarcastically, "how could I have forgotten?"

"I'll have none of your impertinence, my girl! Keep a civil head in your tongue and remember the respect you owe us as your betters."

Bri looked at the duchess and allowed a certain amount of her hatred show through. Then she masked her expression and replied demurely, "Very well, Aunt. You do know what is best."

"Old hag," Greville muttered beside her. Bri had to fight to keep a straight face.

"What was that, Greville?" Lady Corning demanded imperiously.

Greville leveled a charming smile at her that didn't quite reach his eyes. "I said, wise decision, your grace. London is just the answer." The look he sent Bri after this shocking pronouncement nearly had her in stitches.

Lady Corning rose to her feet to signal the ladies to adjourn to the drawing room. Bri sent a look of loathing to Lord Steyne who sat on her other side and firmly removed the hand that was creeping up her thigh. For the first time she could recall, she was relieved to be able to escape with the sharp-tongued ladies.

# Chapter Twelve

Adam had successfully pushed a certain flame-haired, green-eyed countess firmly from his mind. He had succeeded so well, in fact, that he nearly dropped his coffee one morning several months later when he glanced at the social column of the London Gazette.

"Bloody hell," he muttered, much to the amusement of Lord Connor Northwicke who had stopped over that morning.

"Bad news?" he inquired casually.

"Depends on who you are, I suppose," his friend replied cryptically.

Connor reached for the paper and soon saw what has his friend so pensive. "Oh, Lord," he said then.

"Exactly," Adam said almost to himself. "I had tried to tell myself that she would be fine. She was with her family and surely she had exaggerated their treatment of her. Now I wonder."

"As do I," Connor responded thoughtfully. "I had heard, of course, Steyne himself spouting off some rubbish about being engaged to her, but I just thought he was in his cups."

Adam concurred. "I still felt like calling the bastard out," he growled.

"Good thing you resisted," Connor replied dryly. "You'd look no end the fool now if you had given in to your impulse."

Adam did nothing more than grunt in reply.

"And apparently, she is in Town for the Season," Connor added as he turned the page. "Why do you suppose that is?"

"To flaunt her wealth and title?" Adam suggested cynically. "To show us how happy she is to be engaged to Steyne?"

"Or to beg for help to escape?" Connor said softly.

"Oh, yes," Adam scoffed. "That one could be standing on the gibbet with the noose around her neck and she still would tell a man to go to hell if he offered to help her out of it. That's very nearly what happened."

Connor remained silent and watched his friend. He wondered

what thoughts were going through Adam's head. Then he realized that with Bri in Town for the Season, Verena was bound to run into her and his part in keeping Bri's presence a secret would assuredly come to light. It wouldn't be long before she realized who the Countess of Rothsmere was. He groaned.

"What?" Adam asked sharply.

"Nothing," Connor replied quickly as he rose to his feet. He rushed from the room without so much as a goodbye.

Adam watched him curiously, one brow raised. The footman near the door wisely exited before closing it after the retreating Lord Connor.

Any tiny shred of confusion over Connor's erratic behavior was squelched later that afternoon. He entered Adam's study with an apologetic look and opened his mouth to say something but he was forestalled by the avenging fury that exploded into the room right behind him.

"How could you?" Verena, Lady Connor demanded with a decided lack of her usual meekness. "What possessed you to send her back to them? Do you realize who she is marrying?"

"Yes," Adam replied dryly, answering only her final question. He leaned back in his chair and did not bother to rise as good manners demanded he should with a lady present.

Verena stared at him in sudden silence. "She can't possibly want to marry that man," she said firmly but much more calmly. She sat down across from Adam and watched him closely.

Adam was uncomfortable with the situation in which he currently found himself. He had mistreated Verena horribly in the past and he still felt guilty every time he saw her. He wanted to forget that he had misjudged one woman and that alone meant there was a possibility that he had misjudged another.

Connor sat down next to his wife but remained silent. Adam wished he would say something. Or better yet, take his wife and leave.

Verena still stared at Adam. She wanted to rail at him some more for what she felt was a gross injustice on his part. She wanted to tell him that in sending Bri back he had effectively destroyed his only chance for happiness and a measure of inner peace in his life.

For Verena Northwicke strongly suspected that Adam was in love with Bri.

"Do you even realize what you have done?" she asked quietly and with the calm for which she was known. Her violet eyes gazed steadily into his as she awaited his answer.

"I have returned a runaway to her loving family," he replied shortly, playing seriously with the idea of having his closest friends tossed from his home. His tone had come out cold and bitter even to his own ears.

Verena snorted disdainfully. "If you believe that—and I strongly suspect that you secretly don't and are simply trying to convince yourself that you do—you are a far stupider man than I had ever thought," she retorted scathingly. She would have said more but the sudden warning pressure of her husband's hand on her arm stopped her.

Lord Connor had seen the warning glint in Adam's eyes that heralded a setdown that Connor very much feared he would have to murder his best friend over.

"I think it's time we left, my love." Connor's voice held a hint of steel not often heard by his gentle wife. There was never a need. She heard it now, however, and obeyed wordlessly. She rose to her feet after delivering one more look of fury to Adam Prestwich.

But she couldn't resist a parting shot, no matter how hard she tried. She shook off Connor's arm and returned to the large desk behind which Adam still sat. Leaning closer to him she whispered indignantly, "When she is married to that man and must submit to him as a wife must, I hope you realize what you have lost, Adam Prestwich."

Adam dressed for a ball being held by the Earl and Countess of Peterborough's residence a week later. It was to be the opening ball of the Season and it was sure to be a sad crush. Everyone who was anyone would be there.

He didn't know why he was going. Perhaps he hoped it would take his mind off the disastrous news he had received earlier that day from his solicitor.

He tied his cravat into the mathematical, shunning the help of Morris, and managed to get it right after ruining only five starched neckcloths. He stood back and surveyed his appearance critically in the tall mirror.

His black hair was disarranged as usual since he had a habit of shoving his hand through it when agitated; he had been agitated for the whole of that day. His linen was sparkling white and the only relief for the somber black of his coat and knee breeches. Even his waistcoat was dark and he thought that the whole ensemble quite matched his mood. He doubted his attitude would improve much after this night either.

Taking up his cloak since the night was chilly, his hat, and gloves, he stepped out of the house and stepped into his carriage. The coachman drove the short distance from Berkeley Square to Grosvenor where he stopped before Connor's residence. He alighted and entered the house.

He was early, he noted as he glanced at the tall case clock in the entryway. And yet Verena was making her way down the stairs looking very lovely in pale yellow silk with amethysts in her black hair and around her throat. She resembled nothing less than a ray of sunshine.

He bowed and smiled hesitantly at her and received the same greeting in return. She came toward him and smiled again, brighter this time.

"My lady, you are a veritable ray of sunshine," he told her quite sincerely.

"Thank you, Mr. Prestwich," she replied formally with a curtsy. "And you are looking exceedingly handsome this evening."

"If I didn't know how much the two of you actually disliked each other, I may have reason to be jealous," Connor said as he stepped into the hall from the direction of his study. His face was wreathed in a smile of greeting for his friend and one of appreciation for his wife.

Verena went to him and wound her arms around his waist in full view of Adam and the servants and turned a glowing face up to her husband's. "Dislike is such a strong word, Con. I prefer annoy, I think."

She threw a look of amusement over her shoulder at Adam. Con smiled down at her when she returned her attention to him and placed a gentle kiss on her smiling lips.

Adam felt a strange pang in his chest at the tender scene. He realized with a shock that he was jealous. He envied their happiness, their contentment, their peace. It was hard won, he knew, and he could think of no two people more deserving.

And he was so jealous of that joy that it hurt.

His tone came out colder than he had intended. "Perhaps we

should be going, if you are quite through?"

Connor shot him a look of warning mixed with bafflement. Verena stepped away from her husband and flushed as if she just realized what a breach in decorum she had just initiated. Connor saw the look on her face and his expression turned to annoyance when he returned his gaze to Adam. He took her hand, lacing their fingers together and leading her to the door.

Adam offered no apologies or explanations. He just turned around and walked out of the house and into the darkened street.

Lady Rothsmere knew, of course, the moment he entered the ballroom. Adam was with Lord Connor and Doll—Verena. He looked so handsome she felt short of breath. She wished suddenly that she hadn't had to accompany Hadley Steyne this evening.

And she wished Greville had been able to attend. But her cousin had run into some trouble recently and had to avoid Town for the time being.

She didn't realize she was starring until he looked directly at her and their eyes locked. She couldn't look away. It was as if some invisible cord held their gazes motionless. The ballroom receded, the laughing, boisterous crowd dispersed and it was only them.

"Is that not Prestwich? With Beverley?"

The spell was broken. Bri looked away from the magnetic gray-green eyes of her nemesis and turned limpid emerald eyes on her betrothed.

"Prestwich, my lord?" she asked laconically.

Steyne favored her with a hard stare. "Yes, Prestwich. The man who returned you to your family. You know, the gentleman you were just staring at for all of thirty seconds?"

"Only thirty seconds? It had seemed far longer," she said laconically. An hour. All night. A lifetime. She glanced again at Adam but he had moved on and was nowhere in sight.

Beverley? She opened her mouth to ask where Beverley was. Then she realized he must have mistaken Lord Connor for his brother. She supposed this was possible since she had never met the marquess. She supposed they could look alike.

She turned to ask Hadley about his mistake. Then she saw the look of anger on Steyne's face and smiled brightly instead.

Adam stood in the shadows of the ballroom and saw that

smile. It looked suspiciously like the smile of a woman in love. Or at least resigned to her lot in life. He didn't try to understand the rage that threatened to consume him, he just felt it. It was completely unreasonable.

When he had entered the room, he had made a deliberate effort not to look around the room in the hopes of seeing her. He had, instead, lavished praise upon the poise and beauty of his hostess and that of her rather well endowed daughter who was making her comeout this year. The girl in question, Lady Margaret, smiled and flirted with her fan as all young ladies of the *ton* were instructed and he moved on to greet his host.

Then he was done. He could no longer avoid the inevitable. He looked around and saw her—staring at him. He had had to remind himself to breathe. He had had to clench his fist against the sudden searing pain he had felt upon his first sight of her.

She was breathtaking. She wore scarlet silk cut scandalously low across her ample chest. The waist was high as fashion dictated and her hair was piled on her head with a tendril or two allowed to escape. The sleeves of her gown were long and tight ending in a V over her delicate hands and slightly off the shoulder revealing slim and delicately curved shoulders. Adam had to admit that the style was perfect for her.

The color should have clashed horribly with her hair, should have made her pale skin look sallow and unappealing. But it didn't. Her hair seemed to burn like a flame and her skin glowed with health. She seemed to have put on some much needed weight since he had seen her last although she was still quite slim.

He had the sudden urge to place his lips in the curve where her graceful neck met her shoulder. The thought disgusted him. He had no business thinking of another man's betrothed in such a way. Even if she was Steyne's.

How he hated that man! It was a cold, emotionless hatred. Something frightening to behold and worse to feel. He wondered why he felt so strongly after nearly two years. It wasn't as if he were still in love with Carlotta. He was beginning to doubt that he ever was.

"Are you going to stand here in the shadows all night?" Connor asked with a smile.

Adam shrugged and stepped away from the wall upon which he had been leaning. "What else is there to do?" he drawled. He reached down and grasped his quizzing glass in one hand although he did not raise it to his eye. "I have no desire to play cards and dancing holds the same amount of appeal. I am not hungry although a bottle of port would not come amiss. Perhaps I shall take my leave."

Connor laughed. "I'm afraid I can't let you do that, sir. Verena has her heart set on dancing with you, God only knows why, and I find I can deny her nothing tonight."

Adam cast an unreadable look on his best friend. "Do you ever regret your decision?" he asked abruptly.

Connor stiffened slightly. It was not something anyone would have noticed, it was so imperceptible. But Adam had known Connor Northwicke since Eton and he saw the movement. He was treading on dangerous ground, he knew, but it was something he had to ask.

"Do you ever regret getting married? I don't mean Verena in particular, Con, just marriage itself."

The other man relaxed. "Not really. I was ready, I suppose." He turned away from Adam and let his eyes wander over the crowded ballroom until they came to rest tenderly on his laughing wife. "I won't lie and say I wasn't scared out of my mind, but it felt right to marry her. She needed me far more than Lady Mari or any other debutante might have."

Lady Mari was actually Lady Marigold Danvers, the only daughter of Connor's godfather, the Earl of Charteris. He had known her forever and it had seemed natural that they would one day marry. But then Verena had come along and put paid to that notion.

Adam had always wondered what had possessed Connor to court the earl's daughter in the first place. She was a grasping, narcissistic harpy with a malicious streak that had come out after she had learned of Connor's marriage. Adam had been relieved when she had been hounded out of Town last Season for her part in trying to ruin Verena.

Connor glanced at Adam. "There have been very trying times, as you know very well, but the good times have more than made up for them. I recommend marriage to any man with the courage to fight for what he loves." He threw a meaningful look at Adam and strode away, calling over his shoulder, "My wife expects a dance with you, don't forget."

Adam had to smile. He just had to. Verena and he annoyed each other immensely although he actually considered her his friend. And he believed she felt the same about him. He was still smiling as he walked away from his quiet corner and approached her.

# Chapter Thirteen

The peace of the evening failed to reach him as usual. He leaned back in his chair and waited for something, anything to happen to alleviate the constant discontent and restlessness he felt. It was like waiting for death, he thought emotionlessly. Waiting for that ultimate release from life's problems. He almost wished he had the courage—or perhaps cowardice?—to put a bullet through his brain.

Almost. He wasn't quite that far gone in unhappiness to really want to do such a thing. He was merely fed up with the hand life had dealt him. He wasn't ready to fold, but he had the distinct impression that he held a losing hand and that every hand after would hold the same disappointment.

Adam sighed and tipped the decanter at his elbow over his glass for the third time that night. He had been avoiding the real issue ever since his meeting that afternoon with his solicitor. He hadn't wanted to think about that problem. He had naïvely assumed said problem would just go away if he ignored it long enough. But it was still there, haunting his past and trying determinedly to become part of his present and future.

A sudden fit of anger consumed him and he threw his glass at the opposite wall. It shattered into a million tiny shards of crystal and brandy streaked down the paneling.

How dare she try to worm her way back into his life! How dare she try to make him feel guilty for abandoning her! It was far less than she had deserved for what she did to him. Her demands only served to strengthen his feelings that women were nothing more than manipulative sluts and whores who cared for nothing but money and power.

He should have gone to Raven tonight, he thought as his anger disappeared as quickly as it had come. He leaned forward and dropped his forehead into his hand. He really didn't want to deal with any of this right now.

After seeing Bri again after nearly three months of trying to forget her very existence, he was not ready to deal with a past problem who seemed to think she should not be forgotten.

With a muttered oath, Adam rose to his feet and shouted for his horse to be saddled and brought round. He was still in his evening clothes, having gone right to his study and the brandy decanter after the Peterborough's ball. He strode into the hall and paused only long enough to draw on his greatcoat and gloves. Then he disappeared into the night.

Raven had been expecting him. She had heard that Bri was back in Town with her betrothed, Viscount Steyne, as well as the many illustrious titles to whom she was related. The viscount, of course, had been one of Raven's more persistent admirers. She had never really thought of him as dangerous so she assumed that Bri was not being forced into anything distasteful to her.

But Raven also knew that Steyne had a mistress in keeping and she suspected that Bri was not the sort of woman to meekly ignore such an arrangement as ladies were taught to do. Even if she wasn't in love with the viscount.

None of that was to the point. Raven knew that Adam was in love with Bri even if he had yet to realize it himself. She also knew he would come to her, Raven, to try to rid himself of the strange feelings he had toward the countess.

She knew he would come that night. She had heard about his attendance at the opening ball of the Season. She had known that Bri would be there as well.

Raven felt no jealousy, no anger or betrayal. She wanted Adam to be happy. She wanted him to find that certain someone that he deserved more than anything in the world. She was not that person and she knew it. The knowledge did not hurt. It was actually a relief.

For nearly two years, Raven Emerson had been the mistress of Adam Prestwich. For nearly two years, she had enjoyed the time he spent with her. She had enjoyed his conscientious way of teaching her the art of love. She had enjoyed the mindless passion he could arouse in her and the tenderness he showed her despite his tendency to harshness towards women.

But she had secretly despised herself for all of it. She had started out as his mistress with the sole purpose of providing for her ailing father and nine younger sisters. She had not wanted to take a lover when she had first acquired a job on the stage. But necessity had shown her that she was wrong and fate had placed Adam in her path. And so she had agreed to become his mistress.

But now, nearly two years later, at the age of three-and-twenty, Raven was ready for at least a modicum of respectability. She could never be totally respectable, she knew, because of her profession, but she at least wanted to feel respectable.

But she had this evening to get through before any of that could be achieved. She knew her arrangement with Adam was coming to an end soon.

She turned with a smile on her face when she heard his step outside her bedroom door. He opened it and walked in without bothering to knock. When he started to unwind his cravat and shrug out of his coat without saying a word, she knew that the last thing he wanted right now was to talk.

"Have I ever told you about my past?" Adam asked her several hours later.

His tone was bored as if he found the subject tedious in the extreme. Raven mutely shook her head where it rested against his shoulder and waited for him to speak. She had wondered after their third coupling if he would want to talk eventually. There had been a sort of mechanical quality to his lovemaking as if he was only there because he felt he had to.

"I don't know if I'm quite ready to," he murmured candidly. "I try not to think about it, let alone talk about it. Con doesn't even know the extent of my sins."

The extent of his sins?

"I'm a baronet. Were you aware? No? That particular secret Con does know. He is about as good at ferreting out information as I. Sir Adam Prestwich. Awarded for bravery on the field of battle." His tone took on a mocking quality. "Bravery is such a strange quality. If one is wounded on the field, no matter what one's reason for being there, it is brave. Even when the act of a coward is what draws a man there. The man's own cowardice. What a joke."

He had been rubbing his hand up and down her arm and along her shoulder. He suddenly ceased this soothing motion and closed his eyes. He stayed like that for several minutes. Raven began to wonder if perhaps he had fallen asleep when he spoke again.

"I was not exactly discharged with the full goodwill of my superiors," he said in a voice full of self-mockery. "They tend to frown upon an officer, no matter how glorious his battle record, when he participates in a duel with one of his subordinates. Not good *ton*, you know. At least I didn't kill the bastard," he said almost to himself. "He deserved it, I think. But I let him live. And now he plagues me again. Only this time I cannot challenge him. I have no right."

"Steyne," Raven whispered then, the realization dawning on her suddenly. He had fought a duel with Viscount Steyne when on the peninsula. "Why?" She swiveled her head to look up at him.

Adam looked down at Raven as if only then realizing she was even there. His brow furrowed into a frown. "Why what?" he asked tersely.

Raven swallowed hard. She had become rather adept at reading his moods. He was dangerously close to anger, she knew. So, instead of repeating her question, she smiled and snuggled closer to him.

"It was nothing, Adam." She knew he would talk no more that night.

# Chapter Fourteen

Almack's. That holy of holies. The secret—and not so secret—ambition of every debutante ever to grace the London Season. The famous Wednesday night assemblies were presided over by seven patronesses who ruled with a rod of iron. Any lady unfortunate enough to have been involved in a scandal, whether through ignorance, by accident, or quite purposely, was barred from the premises with a hauteur worthy of a queen.

Gentlemen lived by a very different set of rules, of course. A man could be involved in some of the most scandalous situations imaginable and still be welcomed with a smile. After all, everybody loved a rake.

Except Lady Rothsmere.

She stood off to one side of the roped off area of the ballroom and decided that she quite hated the hallowed walls of Almack's Assembly Rooms and wished heartily that she were anywhere else. It was disappointing to say the least. The room was bare of decoration except for the glittering jewelry of the ladies in attendance. The cakes and sandwiches were stale and old and the lemonade and orgeat were weak. The gentlemen often grumbled about the lack of stronger liquids but they were there nonetheless paying court to whichever reigning belle was in Town.

Bri wasn't even comforted by the fact that she seemed to have been deemed one of these belles despite her slightly advanced age and the fact that she was already engaged and her betrothed rarely strayed from her side. She was constantly surrounded by a swarm of gentlemen all vying for her hand in the next dance. They paid her lavish compliments that actually fell upon deaf ears had they but known it. She reacted as any empty-headed debutante might; she simpered and flirted and prayed for death. Or for the night to end, whichever seemed reasonable at the time.

And that was how Adam saw her.

He didn't know why he had allowed Verena to convince him

to come. He hated Almack's. With a passion. There was nothing worse than seeing the marriage mart at its best, or worst, rather. The dance floor was even roped off much like a cattle pen and the young girls making their debuts were paraded around like prize cows for the avid gazes of the gentlemen. It was sickening.

He stood at the edge of the ballroom and watched the young woman he had spent the better part of two years tracking the length and breadth of England. She stood in a circle of men, Steyne hovering at her side with a proprietary air.

Adam leaned back and crossed his arms over his chest, trying to look at her objectively. Was she happy? She certainly appeared to be, he thought, as she playfully rapped one of her gallants on the hand with her fan, a dazzling smile on her lips that didn't quite reach the green of her eyes.

She was certainly in looks, he thought for the second time since he had seen her a few nights before. Her ball gown of clingy emerald silk whispered around her lithe form, flowing over her hips and thighs in soft waves. The neckline was nearly as low as the scarlet dress she had worn before, showing the top halves of two perfect white breasts. A collar of sparkling emeralds and diamonds blazed at her throat with matching earbobs and a diamond tiara in her thick red curls. Her feet were shod in daring gold sandals that laced up her shapely calves.

Adam found himself thinking how much better the entire ensemble would look in a pile on his bedroom floor and had to wonder where the devil such a thought had come from. It was hardly appropriate in the middle of Almack's.

The countess looked over at him then and Adam saw a flash of the spirited beauty he had met for the first time over a year ago when she was working as Verena's maid. Then the sparkle disappeared and she seemed to dull before his very eyes.

He was intrigued. He could not imagine a power on earth capable of controlling the minx that was Lady Rothsmere. He highly doubted it was Viscount Steyne. That cad was too wrapped up in seducing every other man's woman to worry about controlling his own.

Before he quite knew what he was doing, Adam found himself crossing the room until he stood before the one woman who haunted his dreams and every waking moment. He ignored the glowering Steyne and dimly noted that her other gallants seemed to fade into the background.

Bowing, he gave her a dazzling smile and inquired sweetly, "Lady Rothsmere, I hope I find you well?"

"Indeed, I am, Mr. Prestwich. And you?" the countess replied in measured tones.

"I am well," Adam replied, already heartily sick of such an inane topic as the state of their health. What was next? The weather?

Bri regarded Adam Prestwich warily, wondering what he would say next. She could feel the hate emanating from the man next to her and she had to wonder at that as well.

"Would you do me the honor of partnering me for the next waltz?"

She heard the command in Adam's voice and found herself agreeing to dance before Steyne had a chance to cause problems. The countess wondered at the wisdom of allowing the magnetic Mr. Prestwich the chance to converse alone with her, but she had to admit to a certain amount of curiosity.

Placing her gloved hand in his, she allowed him to lead her onto the floor. He put one hand at her waist and drew her close. She felt a tingle go up her spine and found it difficult to maintain her debutante act.

Adam looked down at he girl in his arms and realized how incredibly stupid it was to choose such an intimate dance. He had to stifle the urge to draw her closer until she was pressed full-length against him. He wondered if she felt anything at all. Her amazing eyes were carefully blank.

"You look very beautiful tonight, my lady," he whispered close to her ear. He watched in satisfaction as she started in surprise. Her look was quickly veiled.

"La, sir, you do flatter a girl so," she tittered awfully.

Adam would have cringed had he not been so amused by her purposely shrill voice.

"Nonsense," he replied gallantly. "I only speak the truth."

"Poppycock," Bri said under her breath, unaware that Adam heard. "You do turn a girl's head," she said louder. Was that a note of sarcasm she heard in her own voice?

Adam grinned. "At least you have retained some of that biting wit of which I am so fond," he said lightly.

She gave him a blank look that reminded him of a particularly stupid mongrel dog Connor had once had as a child. It was annoying to say the least.

"What kind of dimwitted female are you?" he said from between clenched teeth and smiling lips.

"Excuse me?" Her lovely eyes filed with tears and her lower lip trembled.

"Oh, good God, Bri! Stop this bloody act. You can't possibly expect me to believe that you are this damned insipid."

"What do you mean?" she asked on a tremulous whisper.

"The devil!" Adam's mask slipped, revealing the cynical and bitter man he really was. "Why did you let them break you, you fool woman?" He executed an elaborate turn in the dance, glaring down at her. When they came out of the turn, she found herself pulled even closer to him. "Why did you let them turn you into an empty-headed chit with nothing to recommend her but a title and fortune?"

"If it wasn't for you, you interfering bastard, I wouldn't even be in this situation," she snapped.

"You're right," he retorted coldly, "you'd be dead."

Unable to deny that very pertinent fact, Bri remained silent, staring at Adam's immaculately tied cravat. Her conscience told her she should be grateful to this very handsome and very enigmatic man. But her anger at having to choose between a madhouse and marriage to Steyne made her foolishly believe that she could have found a way out of that predicament without the help of Mr. Prestwich.

"I'd have contrived," she said half to herself.

"Do you think?" Adam asked, one dark brow cocked in wonder.

Bri was silent for a moment. She knew deep down that she had finally reached the point when she was unable to help herself. When she had sat in that cell all those months ago awaiting her execution, even then she had known that she would never make it out alive.

Of course, she had reckoned without Adam Prestwich. He had swept in like some sort of modern-day Lochinvar and carried her off to safety. It was the stuff romances were made of.

It sickened her. She did not want to feel beholden to this man. He had listened to her story with that insufferably cynical air about him and then turned her over to her fate anyway.

And then he had forgotten about her. The Countess of Rothsmere didn't yet realize that it was this that galled her the most.

With much concentration, Bri replaced her social mask. "Mr. Prestwich, I am feeling faint. Please escort me back to my *fiancé*." She used the word like a weapon although her eyes and face were carefully blank.

"I'll do better than that," Adam replied in clipped accents. "I think you need to get out of this crowd." With that he twirled her out onto the balcony that ran along the back of the building. He was so angry he could barely think straight. He paid no heed to the staring couples who lingered outside to escape the suffocating heat of the ballroom.

Bri barely had time to take a deep breath as Adam swung her around and trapped both hands behind her back. She was pressed intimately against him from chest to thigh. So close, in fact, that she could feel his heartbeat against her breast. Even in the moonlight, she could see the dangerous glitter in his pale eyes and she knew instinctively that she had pushed him too far by mentioning her fiancé.

His head seemed to lower with excruciating slowness and she wondered breathlessly why she didn't simply turn her head away or scream for help. She seemed to be hypnotized by that glittering gaze.

Adam kissed her fiercely; it was almost like a brand. His eyes were open, as were hers, and he watched her closely noting every tiny change in her demeanor. Her breathing quickened, her eyes took on a sparkle and she moaned suddenly low in her throat. He ran his tongue along the seam of her lips and she obeyed his unspoken request almost without thought.

His tongue plunged into her mouth and the fire that seemed to consume her was shocking. She felt his grip on her hands loosen and she reacted more from fear than anger.

Tearing her lips away, she raised her hand and boxed him squarely on the ear.

"What the devil!"

"Do not dare to manhandle me again, Mr. Prestwich," she warned in a breathless, albeit, fierce whisper. "Do so again, sir, and my fiancé will call you out," she added a trifle smugly.

"Not bloody likely," Adam muttered, his eyes narrowed as he

rubbed at his smarting ear. "But at least you sound more like yourself," he added in an undertone, as if his words weren't actually meant for her ears.

Bri softened visibly. "Oh, Adam," she murmured, too distressed to realize she used his given name, "don't you see? I can't—"

"Lady Rothsmere!" called a voice imperiously from the doorway.

Adam stepped away from Bri, realizing he was standing unforgivably close to another man's affianced bride in full view of anyone who cared to look in their direction.

He wondered what she had been about to say.

He wondered what imp of Satan had compelled him to kiss her.

He wondered, with rising pique, if his embrace had at all affected her.

Then she threw him a strangely forlorn and regretful look before her countenance became the bland mask she employed for her family's benefit. He was amazed at the transformation.

"Would you be so kind as to escort me back, sir?" she asked with a smile of false brightness.

He dutifully offered his arm and they joined an older woman of frightening girth and fierce expression who proved to be Lady Rothsmere's duenna. Adam watched them move away and wished suddenly that Almack's served something, anything, stronger than orgeat and lemonade. He needed a brandy. He needed a whole decanter. And perhaps a willing woman beneath him.

He smiled. He would go see Raven, he decided, and spend the night with her. That should exorcise the green-eyed vixen, he was sure. He ignored the voice that insisted it hadn't so far so why would it start now?

He turned toward the door—and found his way firmly blocked by Lord Steyne and two of that man's cronies.

"What business have you with my betrothed, Prestwich?" the viscount asked belligerently.

"The lady and I are old friends," Adam replied softly, somehow managing to convey exactly what sort of friends they were without actually saying anything. He couldn't help needling the coxcomb. He had more reason than just Bri to goad the man. He also felt a malicious desire to punish Bri as well.

He got an elbow in his ribs for his trouble and turned his head to see Connor giving him a reproachful look. Adam looked away and crossed his arms over his chest, giving Steyne such a steady look of contempt that the viscount began to squirm.

"What is this all about, gentlemen?" inquired the strident tones of Mrs. Drummond-Burrell, one of the highest sticklers in the *haute ton* as well as a patroness of Almack's. "If you are going to behave no better than schoolboys, I'll ask you to have the decency to leave. I expected better from you, Lord Connor."

Connor bowed with a devastating smile and assured her that it was all a simple misunderstanding. As usual, his charm didn't fail and the lady moved off after sending a reproving glare towards Adam Prestwich. He just grinned devilishly and offered a somewhat mocking bow. Then he returned his attention to Steyne. The viscount was still watching him with thinly veiled hate.

"So, Steyne," Adam began conversationally—only Connor knew what a tight rein Adam had on his temper, "are you going to call me out? Or do you only take part in duels where *you* have been called out?"

Steyne didn't dare call him out and Adam knew it. After the viscount's ignominious defeat in that duel over two years ago, the man knew better. So he sputtered in anger for a few moments but finally departed. Adam watched him join Bri who was viewing the whole scene with the oddest look on her face. She asked Steyne something and he shook his head. Adam was sure she looked... disappointed.

"If you insist on goading men into duels in the middle of Almack's," Connor said, effectively swinging Adam's attention back to him, "you'll never be allowed in these hallowed walls again."

Prestwich snorted and threw his friend a very un-disappointed look. "I bloody well wouldn't care, Con. A lot of posturing popinjays and dull debutantes were never my idea of a good time. I am surprised I am allowed in here at all, actually."

Connor smiled good-naturedly. "I wonder, am I a posturing popinjay or a dull deb?" He looked up at his taller friend and fluttered his eyelashes.

"Egad!" Adam exclaimed in mock horror. "Do that again and I'll call *you* out."

Connor laughed and clapped Prestwich on the back. "I think

we should leave."

"Will Verena mind?" Adam asked a trifle skeptically. In his experience, the ladies wanted to stay until all hours, dancing and flirting.

"Of course she won't. She's very unfashionable in that she is more mother to our children than the nurse. And she has now been away from them for all of two hours."

Adam knew this but his own experience with the opposite sex led him to believe that such feelings were fleeting if they existed at all. He trusted Connor's wife more than most, liked her even, but old habits are hard to break.

# Chapter Fifteen

Bri sat at her dressing table that night and thought about that kiss. It had shocked her to the core of her being. It wasn't as if she hadn't been kissed before. She had. Those other kisses were better left forgotten. But Adam's kiss was...a glimpse of heaven.

She allowed her thoughts to stray into forbidden territory. What would it be like to, well, to *be* with him? She shook her head. Probably just like being with any other man—extremely unpleasant.

She remembered once telling Doll, Lady Connor Northwicke, that sexual relations between a man and woman could be quite pleasurable. It wasn't that she lied but she truly believed that they had to be despite what nearly every matron had ever said. Raven didn't appear to despise what Adam did to her, after all. She even liked the man despite it.

Bri shoved the thought of Adam and Raven away. It made her bilious just to think about it.

Her own belief had come out in her tone of voice as personal experience, Bri knew, even if she hadn't said so in so many words. She had seen the look on Verena's face before that lady had turned away.

*Am I a fallen woman?* Bri wondered then. The look on Verena's face had said that, although she never mentioned the fact. And Bri knew the belief had comforted her friend somewhat so she couldn't be regretful of the assumption.

Bri turned suddenly as the door to her chamber creaked open. "Brewster, is that you?"

A short laugh greeted her inquiry. A short, male laugh. "No, it is I. Your beloved." Steyne spat the last word as if it were something distasteful to him.

Bri stood and clutched her robe closer to her breasts. "Get out," she said evenly, trying to mask her fear. Was she to be raped even now, when under the protection of her family?

Steyne sauntered closer, his hands shoved in his pockets. "What is there between you and Prestwich, my dear? Anything I should know about?"

"No," Bri said quickly. "I hate that man."

"Do you?" the viscount said mildly. He stopped in front of her and gazed at her intently. "I wonder." He fiddled with the cuff of his shirt, his eyes never leaving her. "You do know what they say about love and hate," he finally uttered into the lengthening silence. It was not a question.

Of course she knew, but she chose not to think about that either.

Bri stared at him haughtily. "It is not proper for you to be in my bedchamber, my lord."

He stared at her for a long moment before replying. He fisted his hands on his hips, then dropped them to his sides, then he crossed them over his chest. His eyes were shuttered and she couldn't read his thoughts. That frightened her more than anything.

"I want something from you," he said finally.

Lady Rothsmere took and involuntary step back. The sudden blaze in his eyes told her exactly what he wanted. "I will scream if you touch me," she hissed through clenched teeth.

"Scream all you want, my dear. It will do you no good."

Bri sucked in a sharp breath. "What have you done to Brewster?" It came to her in a sudden flash that Brewster was more than just her jailer. She was also her protector.

A smile of quite frightening malice curled Hadley Steyne's lips before he took on an expression of false sympathy. "You need not worry that she will interrupt. I have taken care to ensure that she is out for the night."

As soon as the words left his mouth, Bri's feet seemed to grow wings. The viscount was unfortunately between her and the door leading out into the hall but she thought she might be able to reach the dressing room and lock herself inside. Just as she reached for the door handle, she felt a hand grab her nightclothes and jerk her back with enough force to send her sprawling.

The force of her landing succeeded in freeing her from his hold. She scrambled towards the bellpull. He caught her before she had made it ten feet. She wished her room were about a quarter the size it was. Then she might have had a chance of escape.

Then she saw the book on the floor. It was a rather large

volume covered in leather and lying half under the bed. It must have fallen last night when she was reading. Thank God for the laxity of her servants!

With a strength borne of fear and hate, Bri threw the book at her betrothed with all her force. It caught him in the shoulder and he once again lost his hold on her. This time she was able to regain her footing and dash towards the outer door.

She tripped and hit her head on the bedpost.

Steyne rose to his feet with one hand cradling his shoulder and his eyes blazing with rage and hate. With not a trace of gentleness, he hauled her to her feet. She swayed as a wave of dizziness threatened to overtake her. With lightening swiftness, Lord Steyne grabbed her around the waist to steady her and set his lips to hers.

Instead of screaming, Bri nearly swooned again. The man smelled and tasted like strong spirits, stale cigar smoke and sweat and her head was pounding. His hands were on her body and she wished suddenly that Adam had left her to die in Newgate. Anything was better than this!

Even Adam. Oh, God! Her heart and soul screamed out to him, partly in anger and partly in fear. If only life were like the romances. Then her hero would save her before the dastardly villain could steal her virtue.

The viscount's lips left hers for only a moment as he tossed her onto the bed. Bri struggled to sit up and get away from him but her head protested the sudden movement required and he was on top of her and bruising her lips against her teeth again. His fingers fumbled for the edge of her nightgown and then the button of his breeches.

She kicked and hit him, trying desperately to dislodge him. Her fear was quickly becoming an insanity borne of desperation. She had experienced this all before and she knew how painful it was going to be. She couldn't let it happen again.

But it was too late. She screamed then as he entered her body in one painful thrust. She felt and saw the blackness rising towards her and she reached eagerly for it. She slipped into blessed oblivion and avoided the worst of the pain and humiliation.

Or so she thought.

"Bri!"

Adam sat up in bed, the sound of his own voice jolting him

awake. He realized he wasn't in his own bed. A sleepy Raven opened her eyes partially and smoothed her hand over his arm. He looked down at her through eyes glazed with a remembered nightmare.

Even as he sat there, mere moments after waking, Adam could not recall exactly what it was he had dreamed. He knew it had something to do with Bri yet he could remember nothing about it. Almost as if it hadn't really been a dream. More like a feeling. She needed him.

Adam flopped back down on the pillows and stared unseeingly up at the ceiling. Why on earth would she need him, of all people? She hated him. Didn't she?

There was no help for it. He must pay her a call on the morrow and make sure she was all right.

"Oh, dear God!"

Bri came awake to the sound of a tray clattering to the floor. She opened her eyes and looked around groggily. She recognized her room and her maid, Brewster. The woman's face was twisted into a mask of horror.

A puzzled frown crossed her own features before she remembered the events of the night just past. Bri's gaze swung wildly around the room, looking for the source of her pain.

"He's gone, my lady," the maid said in a soothing voice. It was a voice one would use to calm a frightened animal.

Bri returned her gaze to her maid and tried to sit up. The searing pain between her legs made her wince and she nearly gasped.

The reality of her situation came crashing down on her in that moment and she inhaled sharply. She was to be subjected to such horrid treatment for the rest of her life. And she could do nothing about it. Her hand flew to her mouth while the other struggled to pull her nightgown back down over her exposed flesh. She saw blood on the bed, her nightgown, and her legs and struggled to hold back hysterical tears.

Her eyes flew back to the maid. "He-he r-raped me," she whispered, wide-eyed.

Brewster sat on the bed in a major breach of proper servant behavior and gathered the girl in her arms. "I know," she said in the same soothing voice she had used before. "I know. Let it all out, do."

And she did. Brianna Derring, Countess of Rothsmere, wept in the arms of her maid as if her only love had died and she had to face the frightening world alone. She cried until she thought her head would burst. She cried until righteous indignation took over and forced her to dry her tears.

Then she sat back and glared at the window. "This is all his fault."

Brewster stood and went to draw the drapes to let in the early afternoon sun. "Of course it is, my lady. The viscount is a snake, if you'll pardon my saying so."

"Oh, I forgive you, since it's true," Bri replied calmly as she rose gingerly from the bed. She barely winced this time. She moved over to her dressing room to wash and dress. "I wasn't talking about him. I meant Adam Prestwich."

Bri wandered into the drawing room later that afternoon to await the arrival of those gentlemen she had danced with the night before who wanted to pay their respects. She stared at those members of her family already in the room. There was only her Aunt Clara and the woman hired to act as her duenna when Aunt Clara was busy or under the weather.

Mrs. Blodgett was a bulldog type of woman who had a perpetual glare. She invariably treated Bri as if she really were the dimwitted debutante she pretended to be even though the woman knew otherwise. Bri didn't like her in the least.

"Ah, my dear, here you are at last." The viscount came towards her with a smile on his face and his hands outstretched.

Bri managed to suppress the urge to recoil from his touch. She hadn't even noticed him standing near the window. She placed her hands in his and allowed him to kiss her lightly on the cheek.

"Thank you for last night," he murmured into her ear.

She jerked away from him. He released her with a laugh and the look of lust that had just occupied his light eyes disappeared.

She was tempted to tell her aunt what had happened just to see the viscount's look but she knew the futility of such an action. Women had little rights and if it were known that she had been with him, even forced by him, she would have to marry him immediately. As it was, she only had until the end of the Season to try to get out of her predicament.

Mathers, the butler, entered the room to announce the first set of visitors and Bri sat down to receive them.

Adam had, of course, spent an energetic night in the arms of his mistress just as he had decided he would. His heart hadn't been in it, but then, it never had been. And he was discouraged to realize that Bri was as much in his thoughts as ever.

More, in fact. There had been that embarrassing scene when he had awakened from a nightmare only to call for Bri like a besotted schoolboy.

And ever since that blasted dream, he actually felt guilty for having been with his mistress. He felt guilty for his life and all the stupid decisions he had made.

His guilt had led to a confession that even now, later the same morning, he cringed to remember.

"I'm married," he had informed Raven calmly. He could feel her shock in the stiffening of her body as it lay along his. "And she's dying."

He had paused and waited for recriminations, for disgust, anything but the silence of his beautiful companion. He should have known better. Raven was far too perceptive to assume the worst of him.

"Tell me about her," was her reply. He could hear nothing more than curiosity in her husky voice.

Adam laughed, a short, bitter laugh. "I would rather not. I would like to forget her very existence. I don't like that I am reminded of her now. I was foolish enough to believe that if I just pretended she never existed, she would have the decency to disappear. But decency was something she knew nothing about."

Raven had lifted herself slightly so she could look down into his face. She said nothing for a few moments. He just looked back at her. He saw awareness in her eyes and then she was rising from the bed and putting on her silk dressing gown. She knotted the sash securely at her trim waist and tossed a matching, albeit larger, robe at him and left the room.

Adam lay back for a few minutes pondering the perversity of life. Here he was, confessing his sins to his mistress, fully intending to cut ties with her, and she knew it.

He finally rose and donned the gown. He followed the path taken by his mistress and found her in her little sitting room. It was her favorite room, he knew, the room in which she could usually be found.

He had found a glass of port thrust into his hand and then she pushed him into a chair. "Relax," she commanded softly. "Talk when you want. Say what you want. I will listen and it will go no further, Adam. And then you should leave and sort out your life."

Adam stared at her uncomprehendingly. She sighed. "Adam, you need to talk to someone. I am the only one you can talk to right now. You know me well enough to know that I will not judge anything you may tell me and I will not tell anyone else. You also know I will help in any way I can."

She left out the part where he was going to end their association, he noticed. He decided not to mention it either, yet. He settled into his chair and closed his eyes. He didn't want to see Raven's face as he talked.

"Her name is Carlotta. I met her in Spain right after the battle of Vitoria. I fell in love with her and married her. I caught her in bed with another man and left her to her pleasure. After I shot him, that is." He realized his voice was curt, almost defiant. He struggled for calm.

"Steyne was that man."

It wasn't a question, he noticed. "Yes. The bastard deserved far more than he got, I can assure you."

"So you left her there."

"Yes. I returned to Cornwall after the war was over and tried to forget that chapter of my life. Then Boney escaped and I left to fight him again. I was wounded at Quatre Bras and so escaped being in the actual slaughter of Waterloo. I was sent home with a fever and a minor wound."

"And you were awarded for your bravery."

"And I was awarded for my bravery," he growled. He finally looked at her. He wanted to see her reaction to what he was about to say. "I was a coward, my beautiful swan. I was not supposed to be on that field. I was not supposed to be anywhere near it. I was there praying for death."

"You must love her very much."

He had looked for mockery, for contempt, but her face was full of compassion. Damn it, he didn't want her compassion! He didn't want her pity. He wanted her to hate him, to despise him for his weakness. Instead she was watching him with that damned sad look and tears in her eyes.

Adam came to his feet and hurled his glass at the closed door. "I don't love her! I hate her. I wished for death to escape her. To rid myself of her."

"Why did you not simply kill her?" Raven asked calmly. "Or have her killed?"

He stared at her in open disbelief. Was she jesting? She had to be. Raven had not a violent bone in her body.

"Yes, I was jesting," Raven replied with a half-smile, reading his mind with an ease that frightened him. "I needed you to calm down. Please sit." He sat. "You do not love her. But you did once. One does not feel so strongly about infidelity when one is indifferent. And you are not the type to view a woman as your own personal property no matter how much dislike or even liking you hold for her. You feel guilty for having abandoned her, however, and now you plan to bring her here, do you not?"

Prestwich sat in stunned silence for a moment. Then he shook his head slightly and said, "Not here, exactly. I planned to bury her in Cornwall." He chuckled at his ill-chosen words. "Not literally, of course. But she lives in virtual poverty now and I do feel some responsibility towards her."

"Of course," Raven replied evenly as she handed him a new glass. "Now tell me about Lady Rothsmere."

He started. "What about her?"

"You're in love with her, for one thing. You are also planning to give me my *congé* because of her." Her face revealed nothing but acceptance.

"Will you be all right?"

It was her turn to start in surprise. Then she grinned slowly. "Of course I will. I have a small fortune saved. My family and I will survive comfortably if I continue to live frugally. You have been a very generous protector." Her smile faded. "The question is, will you be all right?"

# Chapter Sixteen

*Will you be all right?*

Her question stayed with him all the next day. He heard her voice in his head over and over again.

He had gone early that morning—after only a few hours of sleep—to inform his solicitor of his decision to bring Mrs. Prestwich to England.

He paused in the act of pulling on his boots. Mrs. Prestwich. Or, *Lady* Prestwich, rather. Carlotta. How he had hoped never to hear that name again. How he had hoped never to see her again. But it could not be helped. She was coming to England to live until she died.

Which he was told would be soon. He didn't want to think about her death. He was afraid he would feel relief or even eagerness for the event. He was afraid he would pray for the freedom that it would bring him. He didn't want to feel that way about anyone, not even his wife.

Adam rose to his feet and left his room. He planned to call on Bri to assure himself that she was okay before he left for Cornwall to prepare the way for his wife. His wife. He hated calling her that but that was what she was.

He arrived late that afternoon. The room was still nearly overflowing with gentlemen. Bri sat in the center smiling and laughing just as if nothing had happened between them last night.

Perhaps nothing had.

"Mr. Prestwich, how delightful to see you!" she exclaimed when she caught sight of him. She rose gracefully to her feet and approached him, both hands outstretched.

He took her hands, raised them both to his lips, and bowed. "The pleasure is mine, I assure you," he replied.

He straightened and as he did so, he noticed two things. First, Steyne was there with a smug look on his face even while his eyes blazed with hatred for Adam or Bri, maybe both. It was hard to tell.

Second, something in Bri had changed overnight.

He wasn't sure what it was. There was an anger in her eyes that was all for him, he knew. That was not surprising. He had often been informed of her dislike of him. But there, in the back of her eyes was a wariness, a fear even, that had not been there before. It reminded him of something but he was unable to recall the memory that hung just on the edge of his recollection.

He smiled charmingly at her. "And how goes your morning?" he asked politely.

"Very well, indeed," she murmured with false brightness. "What more could a girl want than a roomful of gallant young men eager to bow to her every whim?"

There was a cheer from some of her devoted swains at this pronouncement. She smiled sweetly at them and then turned her hard emerald eyes back to Adam. He was taken aback at the new emotion in her eyes. It was...a plea for *help*? No, it couldn't possibly be. He pushed the thought away.

His visit was over in the regulation ten minutes. Bri watched him rise to take his leave and felt a mixture of longing and relief. She had to quell the urge to stop him and beg for help. She knew instinctively that he would do everything in his power to help her if she only asked. He was an honorable man. He would do so for any girl in distress no matter how much he disliked her.

But she was relieved that he was leaving. She had been so tempted to blurt out that she hated him for what he had allowed to happen to her the night before and for what would be happening to her for the rest of her life. She wanted to tell him that it was all his fault and he should have left her to die in Newgate with her pride intact.

With her pride intact? Even Bri had to admit that to die at the end of a rope was not an act of pride. In her case, it was an act of cowardice. It was also humiliating and degrading.

Much like last night was. Humiliating and degrading.

As she sat in the crowded drawing room, surrounded by people, it hit her again. Last night, she had been raped. A man had come into her room and taken his pleasure of her against her will. He had invaded her body and caused her the worst pain and humiliation she had ever known.

She wasn't even sure what was so different from this rape than the others she had experienced. Perhaps it had something to do with the fact that a *gentleman* had never before raped her. They were supposed to protect ladies, not attack them.

She actually couldn't count how many times she had been raped but she had never felt this sense of fear and helplessness. The other times she had just lain there and let it happen, she had never fought as she did last night. Throughout it all, she had had the feeling that she could escape again. All she had to do was run. All she had to do was leave. This time, she was trapped.

A sob escaped her before she quite knew it was coming. She looked down quickly and tried to stifle the tears that longed to follow. She needed to escape. She wanted to have another good cry.

"Lady Rothsmere? I wonder if perhaps you would care to stroll with me on the terrace?"

Bri looked up into Adam's face. She tried to smile but knew it was a hopeless effort. "Thank you, sir," she replied instead.

She rose to her feet and laid her hand on his proffered arm. She ignored everyone as he led her through the open French doors and onto the terrace beyond. He released her and handed her a large handkerchief as soon as they were out of sight of the guests in the drawing room.

"I was right," he said softly. "There is something very wrong."

Her head snapped up, all her fear and distress replaced by an unreasoning anger. "There is nothing wrong. If there was anything wrong, Mr. Prestwich, you can hold yourself accountable. Had you minded your own business and stayed out of my life, I would be fine. I would be happy. I would…"

"You would be dead," Adam retorted bluntly. His own feelings of guilt rose to the surface and he lashed out at her. "If you were not such a headstrong, spoiled brat, you would be far better off! I almost feel sorry for Steyne. He will stuck with you for the rest of his life."

Her hand seemed to fly of its own accord. He easily caught it and held it in an iron grip. "You will not strike me again, my lady," he said in measured, even tones. "You will not blame me for your own stupidity, either. You will take responsibility for your actions." He released her hand and stepped back. "And I will take responsibility for mine," he added very softly.

He performed a rather stiff bow, turned on his heel and took his leave by way of the garden path. Bri watched him go, not realizing that she still clung to his handkerchief as if it were the last thing of value in her life.

Blast the woman! He should not be feeling guilt for returning her to where she belonged. He should not feel the need to beat Steyne to a pulp if he dared hurt her. He shouldn't feel this overwhelming urge to kiss her senseless just to prove that she was not indifferent to him.

Oh, but she wasn't indifferent, he admitted sardonically as he climbed into his phaeton. She was far from indifferent. She hated him.

And he wanted her. God, how he wanted her. He would not admit even to himself that he loved her. Raven was wrong. What he felt for Bri was nothing more than lust. He could not possibly love such a headstrong, willful, infuriating young woman.

He pulled to a stop in front of his mansion and leapt down. He entered the house and told the butler to make sure his curricle was ready to go in the morning, early. He didn't even bother telling him where he was going. It was really none of the man's business.

As Adam entered his room and stared unseeingly at his reflection in the mirror, he remembered the look in Bri's eyes when he had bowed over her hand. At the time, he had not wanted to notice. He had even told himself he was wrong. But after exchanging such heated words with her, words that she obviously believed, he could not longer ignore it. And he knew the truth of it before the word had even fully formed in his mind.

She had looked, she felt, betrayed. By him.

Adam Prestwich left Town early the next morning without informing even his best friend. Only his solicitor and his now former mistress knew his destination, knew that he had even left. He preferred it that way. He didn't want anyone following him and discovering his best-kept secret.

He was running. And he knew it. And he hated himself for it even as he told himself it was necessary. He had to arrange things for Carlotta and he had to get away from Bri. He had to sort out his feelings and come to terms with his past. And he needed the time alone to do it.

She would probably arrive within the month. He had approximately four weeks or so in which to examine his heart and mind. It was something he was not looking forward to. Like a visit to the toothdrawer. He grimaced.

Adam may have been considered an absentee landlord since most of his time was spent in London or Denbigh where he had practically grown up. But he had a very reliable steward who happened to be a relative and he was respected by his tenants since he was not too high-in-the-instep to work alongside them when he happened to be around for the planting season or the harvest.

The estate had actually only been his for a little over three years. He had only become aware of the fact after Toulouse when he had returned home in some disgrace. He had been disgusted with the extent of decay in which he found his family home. His father's debts had been every bit as bad as he had suspected.

He was never more thankful for the fortune he had amassed than at that moment. He hired Miles Prestwich as steward and the man had proven invaluable. Between the two of them, they were able to return the estate to its former prosperous glory in record time.

Adam arrived in Cornwall a few days after his departure from London. He strode into the house, much to the surprise of West, the butler, and Miles, who was crossing the hall as Adam walked in.

"Adam!" Miles smiled in welcome and walked forward, extending his hand as he did so. The cousins shook hands, both smiling. "What brings you home?"

Miles was a well-favored young man with dark hair and an open, friendly countenance. He had Adam's height but lacked his broadness. Adam had thought upon first meeting him that if Connor and himself could be combined into one person, the result would be Miles. Adam had always liked Miles. It was actually hard not to.

"I have some things to take care of," Adam replied evasively. Miles led the way into the study, which was located on the ground floor of the Elizabethan mansion.

Adam removed his greatcoat, threw his hat and gloves on a table, and sat down in a large leather armchair with a deep sigh. "It's good to be home," he said almost without thought.

Miles's eyebrows shot up. "That's not what you usually say," he remarked in surprise.

Adam frowned. "Well, I say it now," he replied dismissively.

Miles shrugged and sat down after pouring two bumpers of

brandy and handing one to his cousin. "Will you disclose the nature of your business? Or must I wait until the very last moment, as usual, and try to adjust accordingly?"

Adam threw him a look, half annoyed, half amused. "Is that what I usually do?" he asked.

"Usually," Miles admitted candidly.

"I see."

"I don't think you do," Miles murmured. He sipped his drink thoughtfully. "Do you realize what a strain it is to try to accommodate every possible outcome of a situation of which you know absolutely nothing?"

Adam's brows shot up this time. It was interesting to see his cousin with a glass of brandy, a sight he'd never before beheld. The man must indeed be under a great deal of strain.

Adam remained silent for a moment, downed his brandy, set the glass aside, and rose to his feet. "I think I will wash the travel dust from my person. See you at dinner?"

Miles sighed. "Very well, Adam." He rose to his feet and bowed. "I'll see you at dinner."

# Chapter Seventeen

While Adam played gentleman farmer in the wilds of Cornwall, Lord Connor Northwicke sat behind the desk in his study in Grosvenor Square two weeks later taking care of some paperwork. His wife, Verena, sat curled up in a chair by the fire reading the latest book by that anonymous author who was revealed as a young lady of gentle birth by the name of Jane Austen. The couple often spent mornings in this companionable way before having to dress to receive visitors and today was no exception.

Until Samson entered to inform my lord that there was a gentleman below desirous to speak with him on a matter most private.

Connor raised one eyebrow imperiously. It was too early for social calls. He rose to his feet and took the card from the tray held by the butler. The corner was carefully turned down to show that the visitor had called in person. Lord Connor stared at the name with a frown between his brows. He didn't know the Earl of Greville.

"A private matter, you say?"

"Yes, my lord. And most important."

"I suppose I should see him then," Connor said in resignation. "Where have you put the earl?"

"In the library, my lord."

Evidently, the earl had passed muster with Samson, who was known to throw pretentious mushrooms out on their ears if they had the temerity to request an interview with the new Marquess of Beverley. Connor filed this surprising development in the back of his mind as he turned to his wife.

"I'll be back soon, my love. This should not take long." He dropped a kiss on her cheek and left the room.

He entered the bookroom unseen. The man standing by the window was a stranger to him—and definitely a gentleman. His maroon jacket stretched across very broad shoulders without a crease. It had the look and feel of Weston's tailoring. Buckskin breeches encased legs of solid muscle and tucked into shining boots made by Hoby. The man was taller than himself, although perhaps not as tall as Adam's six-feet-two-inches. He appeared younger and was a good bit broader in chest and shoulder—and Connor suspected Greville owed none of it to padding.

Connor had to suppress a shiver of unease as he hoped the earl's business was friendly. The man was a veritable Goliath.

As if sensing his presence, Greville turned. Connor took in boyishly handsome features twisted into a worried frown, curly brown hair, dark brown eyes, and a white waistcoat. The earl bowed and stretched out his hand in greeting.

"Lord Connor, I presume?" His voice was a deep baritone, matching to perfection his impressive physique.

"I am." Connor took the proffered hand. "And you are Lord Greville. Welcome. Have we met?" He gestured for his guest to be seated and offered a brandy, sensing that the younger man's business was just as important as Samson had believed.

Greville accepted and waited in agitated silence as his host poured the drinks. He presently had a glass in hand and he downed the contents in one swallow. Connor raised his eyebrows at this and silently refilled the earl's glass. Greville smiled apologetically.

Connor sat down opposite his guest and smiled encouragingly. "Perhaps if you explain your problem, you may find some relief."

The earl consumed his second brandy slower and apologized for his obvious agitation. "I have come on behalf of my cousin. She confided in me once that the marchioness, your wife, is her particular friend. I thought perhaps you would be willing to help."

"And who is your cousin, my lord?"

"Greville, please," insisted the younger man. Connor inclined his head. "My cousin is Lady Rothsmere."

"Bri is the cousin for whom you are seeking help? It is true that she and my wife are or were, rather, particular friends. But they have not seen or spoken to each other since Bri's return to Society. My wife has been banned from visiting her or speaking with her for reasons unknown to either my wife or I. May I inquire as to why you feel the countess needs our help?"

"Certainly, my lord. My distress is caused by her engagement to Viscount Steyne. The man is a snake and a cheat and a scoundrel of the worst kind. An alliance with him is not to be borne!" he ended emphatically.

"Calm yourself, Greville." Con studied him for a moment and wondered where this hotheaded youth had been when Bri really needed him. He seemed to be the only relative with any sort of friendly feelings toward the countess, yet Bri had never mentioned him.

"A lot of betrothals and marriages are sometimes less than one had at first hoped for," he finally replied, thinking of the early stages of his own marriage, "and as much as I dislike Steyne and feel Bri is better off with someone else, there's really nothing we can do. She entered the betrothal of her own volition, Greville. To get involved would be dishonorable."

"The devil it would!" the young lord exploded. He rose from his chair and clenched his hand so tight that the fragile crystal glass in his hand shattered. He was so incensed, he failed to notice the blood or the tiny shards of glass imbedded in his palm. "If you believe she is willing, then you are just as blind as the rest of Society and twice as heartless considering you claim friendship with her!"

"Careful, Greville," Connor warned softly as he too, rose from his seat. He took the earl's hand and examined it for serious cuts as he continued in the same soothing tone, "If you're not careful, I'll have to call you out. And I'd hate to put a bullet in you since I find I quite like you despite your temper."

Satisfied that he had removed the last piece of glass, Con wrapped his handkerchief around Greville's hand after applying a salve that he kept handy for just such small emergencies. Then he rang for Samson to clean up the glass.

The butler arrived and directed the little maid set to the task. Then he bowed and withdrew.

Connor gently pushed the earl back into his seat before resuming his own. "Now, explain your insult, please." Adam would have been surprised to hear the note of command again in such a relatively short period of time.

Greville recognized the note of authority and reacted automatically to it as most men did despite their size or station in life. "Bri was given a choice, Lord Connor. She could either marry Steyne or live out the rest of her days in a madhouse. She saw the viscount as the lesser of two evils." He looked down at his bandaged hand without really seeing it. "It took a great deal of prodding to get her to tell me this. I have had to rescue her from a madhouse once already."

Connor digested this bit of news with a grim expression and a sinking feeling of unease that Greville told the truth. He also believed the man didn't exaggerate. He felt Adam should be informed but he had to know a few things first.

"Why Steyne? I doubt a prospective husband was simply chosen out of the clear blue sky."

"Indeed," the earl replied calmly. The only sign that he was still agitated was the compulsive movements of his left hand while he tugged and fiddled with the bandage on his right. "From what I can gather from Bri and overheard conversations, I have deduced that Steyne is holding something, a secret of some sort, over all our heads, like a veritable sword of Damocles. It's serious enough that my uncle is willing to part with most of Bri's fortune to keep the cad silent. Would that I knew what the secret was and somehow prevent Bri's sacrifice!"

"Is there anything else I should know?"

"Only that she has some strange bruises on her neck and arms that she tries to hide. She told me she fell, but I think Steyne or perhaps Uncle is beating her. I can't get her to admit it, though. She insists that she fell."

Connor's grim look increased if such a thing were possible. Adam would definitely have to be told. "Adam Prestwich could and would help," he replied without any qualms about volunteering his absent friend.

"I bloody well don't need that bastard's help," Greville said darkly.

"That *bastard*," Connor returned with deadly quiet, "is my closest friend. And I don't take friendship lightly."

"He could have helped her escape—I know he has the money to do so—but he returned her instead, effectively signing her death warrant," the earl retorted angrily.

Connor leaned toward him. "Listen well to what I am about to tell you, puppy, for I'll not repeat myself. Prestwich tracked Lady Brianna Kai Derring, Countess of Rothsmere, for more than three years. His search intensified over the past year after he inadvertently discovered her working for my wife. His search finally ended here in London. She was awaiting execution in

Newgate Prison for petty theft. Yes, you should stare, my young friend. She didn't tell you that, did she?

"Bri was half-starved and looked like any poverty stricken woman from the streets; I doubt she has managed to retain her virginity, she has certainly lost her innocence. Adam bought her freedom and took her to his own home to nurse her back to health after she contracted a fever. He has saved that girl twice. He had to return her since she is underage. The law is on your uncle's side and Adam has not the power to fight two dukes and an earl in court."

"She stayed alone with him in his home?" Greville said in tones of disbelief and rising excitement. "Then he had compromised her. Honor demands he marry her!" he concluded triumphantly.

"You would have him marry her? When just a few moments ago you seemed to think him of a level with Steyne?"

"Anyone is better than the viscount," Greville replied. "Will Prestwich marry her, do you think? Will he have to be forced?" The young lord seemed to relish the prospect of "forcing" Adam's compliance.

"Bloody hell, you know Adam Prestwich not at all," Connor remarked mildly. "If he is forced to marry Bri, the hell she would have known with Steyne would be as heaven compared to life with Adam."

"And yet you claim him as friend," the earl retorted.

"The very best," Connor agreed benignly. "He is the best of men to have in a pinch, trust me. He does, however, hate to be forced and his dislike of manipulative females is legendary. You really don't want to force his hand."

"Perhaps not," Greville conceded grudgingly. "But she can't marry Steyne either. He would destroy her."

"Why have you not helped her?" Lord Connor asked curiously, ignoring his inclination to avoid asking impertinent questions.

The earl flushed in embarrassment but answered the question anyway. "I have tried. I mentioned helping her escape the madhouse. But I lack the funds and power to help her in any lasting sort of way."

"Very well," Connor replied shortly, coming to a sudden decision. He rose to his feet, paced the room once, and returned to stand before his guest. He stared down at him thoughtfully. "I don't know where Adam is. And his butler won't know either. He has a habit of just disappearing without a trace. His solicitor will know but even I can't get such information out if that clam. There is only one other person who may know his whereabouts." He smiled and bowed. "I would be honored if you would accompany my wife and I to the theater tonight, Greville."

"In Drury Lane? Why?"

"I will explain afterwards. First, say you will accompany us."

# Chapter Eighteen

Levi, Lord Greville, listened to Lord Connor speak to his wife as they were leaving that night.

"I would like you to stay with Aunt Amelia directly after the show."

"Why?" the beautiful marchioness asked curiously.

The marquess smiled. "Greville and I must pay a visit to the green room and you know it is not a place for ladies."

Lady Connor grinned. "Thinking of setting up a mistress, my love? How very...*tonnish* of you, to be sure."

Greville looked from one to the other, caught a wink from the aunt directed his way and relaxed. Apparently, this type of conversation was a normal occurrence for this particular married couple.

The play was Shakespeare's *Romeo and Juliet*. The woman playing Juliet was breathtakingly beautiful with very long, very straight black hair that hung loosely down her back almost to her knees. Her eyes were dark and slightly tilted giving her a sleepy exotic look.

Greville wondered if she had a protector. He wished he had the means to take her up. The thought occurred to him that perhaps Northwicke *was* there to set up a mistress. Perhaps he had his eye on the dark exotic girl. But of what possible help would that be to their cause?

The play finally ended, not that anyone in their party particularly wished for it to end such was the talent of the woman Greville discovered was known as the Ebony Swan. But end it did and Greville soon found himself in the green room with the marquess, standing before the delectable Swan.

Greville glanced at Northwicke as he bowed to Miss Raven Emerson. Then he turned and bowed as well.

"Might we have a word with you in private, Miss Emerson?" the marquess asked then with a devastatingly cajoling smile.

She smiled faintly, looking a trifle annoyed, Greville thought, and rose to her feet and beckoned them to follow her, leaving a very disappointed court of admirers behind.

"We won't take but a moment of your time," Connor assured her as the door to her private dressing room closed behind them.

"Very well," she replied, her offstage voice airy and light with a slight huskiness that caused an instant physical reaction in Greville. He wondered again if she already had a protector.

They seated themselves and Lord Connor explained that they were looking for Adam since they were in the way of having some information that that man would be vastly interested in.

Her dark brows rose in surprise. "Was I the last to see him?" she asked then, looking from one gentleman to the other in sudden consternation. "That was nearly two weeks ago."

"As to that, I'm not sure," the marquess replied carefully. "Other than I, in whom he didn't confide his intentions to leave Town, you are the one he is closest to. I thought perhaps he might have mentioned his leaving."

Greville watched the worried look deepen on her face before it changed to an expression of sadness. He wondered what earth-shattering secret they were about to be made privy to.

She smiled ruefully. But her rueful smile turned quickly into a frown. "Does this have anything to do with Lady Rothsmere?"

Connor nodded. "Have you noticed something, anything?"

"Only that she is in some sort of trouble that has escalated beyond her control. Adam asked me to keep an eye on her before he left. I have noticed the fear with which she looks at her betrothed. It is not natural even in an arranged alliance such as her ladyship's obviously is."

"Do you have any idea what the problem may be, what is causing her fear?" Greville asked.

Miss Emerson turned the full force of her seductive gaze on him. She stared at him wordlessly for a moment before replying. "I really couldn't say. I would hate to accuse him of raping her but I have seen that particular type of fear before in several of my more unfortunate fellow actresses. She does not appear broken, however, my lords. She has an unusual amount of spirit, I think."

"I will convey your information to Adam," the marquess said grimly. "Where is he?"

"He is in Cornwall, gentlemen. And, incidentally, he has

broken off his association with me so that is the extent of the help I am able to provide, I'm afraid. I highly doubt he will be confiding in me any longer."

Greville had felt his heartbeats pick up a pace at her pronouncement and she again met his eyes. The dark depths held an invitation he would be a fool to ignore. Indeed, he decided impulsively, he would not ignore it.

The express was sent off. Now all they could do was wait and watch. If something happened between now and Adam's return to London, they would have to act without him. Connor hoped that would not be necessary.

Verena demanded to know what was going on. She cornered him in his study and refused to take no for an answer. Connor reluctantly told her, omitting to mention the possibility of rape. His wife was indignant enough as it was. She didn't need a reminder of her own traumatic past.

"You have to do something," she told him unnecessarily. "You can't let them do this to her."

The marchioness was pacing back and forth in front of him like a caged panther. She paused to glare at him. "Well?"

Connor stood before her and had to fight down a grin despite the seriousness of their topic of conversation. He crossed his arms over his chest and raised one pale brow. "Well, what?"

Two small fists came up and planted themselves on her hips. "What do you plan to do?"

"I sent for Adam."

Verena became very still. "You...*what?*" she asked in a deceptively mild tone of voice.

"I sent for Adam. He is the best one to help, you know."

"No, I'm sure I don't know. Bri hates him and well you know it. And he isn't particularly fond of her either. Why would he so far extend himself to help her now?"

Connor shrugged. "Probably because he loves her," he replied carelessly.

Verena released a snort of laughter. "You must be jesting! Or foxed. Are you foxed?"

He smiled. "No, Doll, I am not foxed. Just observant. And I seem to recall a comment you made to Adam in regard to his losing something of value before he'd even found it."

She bristled. "Meaning I'm not? Observant, I mean. And I only said that to needle him. I didn't really believe it."

Her husband's brows snapped together. "You are very prickly of late. Are you increasing again?" He almost laughed when she blushed. He did smile. "Another set of twins?" he asked hopefully.

"Good Lord, I hope not," she exclaimed with a mock grimace. "The set we have are enough. A single child would be most welcome, though."

Connor grinned at her and took her in his arms. She snuggled into his chest and sighed. He kissed her dark curls and murmured, "Stay out of this situation with Bri, my love. Especially now."

She stiffened but her voice was calm. "You can't stop me from trying to help my friend, Con. You won't stop me."

The marquess drew away from her and stared down into glittering violet eyes. His expression was as stern as his voice. "You will obey me in this, Verena."

She jerked away. "And if I don't?" she challenged recklessly.

"You'll be sorry."

Her little chin went up a notch and her arms crossed over her chest. "Are you threatening me? Will you beat me, Con?"

Connor's blue eyes grew hard. "I won't beat you," he replied evenly. "But I do believe you realize that it is in your best interest to stay as apart from this as possible."

Verena noticed the tone of his voice changed and took on that implacable "lord of the manner" quality. She dropped her hands and looked away. "I will obey you," she responded with the utmost reluctance.

"I do need your help," her husband added gently. Her eyes flew up to meet his. "It will be nearly a week before Adam can get here. All we can do until then is wait and watch. And hope that nothing happens to set our plans in motion before Adam arrives."

"What can I do, my lord?"

Connor threw her an exasperated look. "Don't do that, Doll."

"Do what, my lord?" she asked innocently.

"Don't 'my lord' me. I hate it when you do that."

"I apologize. What can I do, Lord Connor?"

Her very patient husband exhaled in annoyance but didn't respond to her goading. He had discovered to his amusement and chagrin that his meek little Doll wasn't so meek when she was increasing. "I need you to be there for her. I think she will need a friend. But you have to act as though all is well. I don't want Steyne suspecting anything. He's unpredictable enough as it is."

Adam read the blasted letter again. It was unnecessary for him to hold it in front of his face as he did since he had already read it so many times he nearly had it memorized.

The message was clear. Bri was in trouble. She needed him. Again. And of course, he would run to her rescue. Again.

He had to return to London as soon as possible. Tomorrow morning, in fact. Maybe even tonight. He would have to inform Miles of Carlotta's arrival after all, then. She'd arrive in less than two weeks. He had hoped to leave it until the last possible moment just as Miles accused him of doing habitually.

Adam leaned back in his chair and closed his eyes. He tossed the letter on the desk in front of him. He didn't want to tell Miles. But he had to help Bri. Connor had neglected to disclose exactly what was wrong. But Adam knew his friend well enough to know that it was nothing trifling. The man was actually requesting Adam's return to Town after all. It had to be serious.

Life or death, Adam thought as his eyes snapped open. He sat up and stared unseeingly ahead of him. Damn. It had to be life or death. Connor would never have asked him to return else. He would have handled the situation himself.

Adam drew a frustrated hand through his black hair. Then his hand knotted into a fist and slammed down on the desktop.

"Bloody hell!"

Adam walked to the door, threw it open, and strode into the hall bellowing for Miles. The steward appeared in the doorway of the library with a look of question on his pleasant countenance.

"Follow me and listen carefully," Adam commanded curtly as he continued on his way to his bedchamber. Miles Prestwich dutifully fell into step beside him. "My wife is due to arrive in less than a fortnight. Prepare the Rose chamber for her and send for the doctor to attend her. She is dying. Tell no one who she is. If anyone asks, she is merely a relative of some sort. I'm sure you can fill in the details accordingly."

He ignored his cousin's openmouthed astonishment and shouted for Morris. The valet appeared in the bedroom, stood looking at his master for all of two seconds, and disappeared again. Adam turned and left the room with his cousin close beside him.

"Any questions?"

Miles swallowed uncomfortably. "Should she die before your return…" he trailed off in question.

Adam stopped and stared at him. In truth, although he knew she was dying, Adam hadn't actually considered her *death*. He did now, albeit dispassionately. "Bury her," he replied laconically.

"B-bury her?" Miles said faintly. "Just like that? Your wife? Adam, your *wife*?"

Adam sighed. "I haven't the time for explanations, Miles. She is my wife, yes. Unfortunately. It was a mistake to marry her and that's all I will say about it. Her name is Carlotta. Carly. Call her what you like. I doubt she'll care." He resumed walking towards the front of the mansion.

West appeared as if from nowhere. "Send for my racing curricle and the blacks. Have them out front immediately." West bowed and shuffled off.

Adam turned around. Miles was watching him with the same look of astonished horror that was on his face when Carlotta was first mentioned. He sighed and took his cousin by the arm. In moments they were back in the study. He pushed Miles into a chair and poured him a brandy.

"Drink this and tell me what's going through that fertile imagination of yours," Adam said curtly.

Miles looked up at him with wide eyes. "When did you get married?"

Adam frowned. "It must be nearly three years ago. Why does that matter?"

The steward shrugged and looked into his glass. "Makes it all seem a little less fantastic just knowing that one simple detail."

"Indeed? Wait until you meet Carly," Prestwich responded dryly.

# Chapter Nineteen

"How dare you deny visitors to me!" Bri raged at her Uncle, the Duke of Corning, late one evening. "Lady Connor Northwicke is my dearest friend. I will not have her denied admittance."

The duke raised one haughty brow and gave her a look of contempt. "I will deny whomever I choose, Brianna. The marchioness has a shady past to say the least, according to her father and I'll not have you associating with her."

"I will see whomever I choose, *your grace*. I am mistress here whether you like it or not. If you feel the need to ride roughshod over someone, go to your *own* home and order your *own* servants around."

Bri knew she hit a sore spot with the duke. He was so short of the ready that he had no townhouse of his own. He had no servants to order around. He was dependent upon her.

But he also had control of her money. And for the time being, her life.

The old man rose slowly to his feet and towered over her. His voice was filled with deadly menace. "Beware, Brianna Derring. I will not tolerate impertinence. Remember what I told you."

She heard a strange whirring in her head and fought the blackness that welled up. She couldn't faint now. She wouldn't let him know how he frightened her.

She straightened. "I will see the marchioness." She turned to leave. "Denbigh is her father-in-law, you know," she threw casually over her shoulder. "I have heard he is very protective of her."

She closed the library door very softly behind her and was rewarded with the sound of breaking glass on the other side. A slow smile of genuine satisfaction spread over her face.

Verena was disappointed and not a little worried when she was turned away from Bri's door earlier that afternoon. But she wouldn't let herself feel discouraged. She was determined to see her friend.

Lady Connor returned the next day at the time deemed proper to pay calls. She was admitted this time and actually asked to step into a small private room to await the countess instead of being simply shown into the drawing room with the rest of the visitors. She declined the offer of tea and the footman withdrew after bowing deferentially.

Verena sat down and looked around curiously. The room was very small considering the size of the house. It was lovely, though. The furnishings were delicate and very feminine. Verena was charmed by the shades of pale yellow, blue, and green that dominated the room. It had the peaceful quality of a field of daffodils bathed in the afternoon sun.

The door opened to admit the Countess of Rothsmere. The two young women stood and stared at each other for what seemed an interminable amount of time. Then a tear escaped Bri's green eyes to trail miserably down her pale cheek and she found herself being hugged tightly.

"Tell me what has happened," Verena commanded softly as she led her to a settee and pulled her down onto it.

Bri wiped the tears away with a tiny scrap of lace and gave her friend a watery smile. She held up the now wet scrap and said, "Useless. I don't know why we ladies carry these minuscule little scraps of lace around and insist on calling them handkerchiefs." She thought longingly of the larger one that now resided under her pillow.

Verena smiled sadly. She reached for her hand and held it tightly. "Do you need help?" she murmured gently.

It was the wrong thing to say. She realized it as soon as the words were out of her mouth. The countess sat straighter and her chin lifted. Her tears dried instantly. It was as if she hadn't even been crying. Then she smiled with false brightness.

"Help? Whatever are you talking about, Doll? I am engaged to a handsome gentleman"—did she stumble over the word?—"who adores me and I have my loving family."—She definitely gritted her teeth over that one—"What more could I want or need?"

Verena shrugged and glanced down at their linked hands. She knew something was wrong. The countess was squeezing her hand painfully tight and didn't even seem to realize it.

Bri disengaged her hand and rose to her feet. "Shall I ring for tea?" She crossed to the bell pull without waiting for an answer and jerked it rather violently.

Verena said nothing about having declined the footman's offer of tea and allowed Bri to order a tray. She hoped the normality of taking tea together would allow them to regain some of their lost time together. *Perhaps Bri will then trust her enough to ask for help.*

They sat in silence until the tray arrived. It wasn't necessarily an uncomfortable silence but there was some undeniable tension.

Bri poured and handed her friend a cup without first asking if she would even like one. This action was unusual considering the last time they had spoken, Bri had been Verena's abigail. Lady Connor's worry deepened.

The marchioness strove for a topic that would relax her friend. Bri saved her the trouble.

"How is Lord Connor? Oh, but he is Beverley now, of course. How is he?" Bri's smile was bright and her eyes were blank of anything but curiosity.

"He is well. He refuses to use the title. You heard about his brother?" Verena asked a trifle reluctantly. It was not a subject she cared to talk much about.

"Only recently I was told that he died leaving Lord Connor Denbigh's heir. Why should he refuse to be known as Lord Beverley?"

Verena looked down at her hands, which trembled slightly. She carefully set her cup and saucer down before replying to Bri's remark. When she did, she was glad to note the emotionless quality of her voice.

"Beverley died suspiciously in France. I was living with Amelia, Connor's aunt, when we heard of it." Then she waited for the inevitable question.

Bri's face took on a puzzled frown. "Living with Connor's aunt? Where was Connor?" She paused briefly but hurried on. "Oh, don't answer that, please. It was very impertinent of me to ask. Forgive me."

"There's nothing to forgive, Bri. You are my friend."

She left it at that. She picked up her teacup and sipped cautiously, willing her hands to be still. It amazed her how much certain memories still affected her.

Verena closed her eyes. She felt her cup being lifted from her suddenly nerveless fingers and her hand was tightly encased in Bri's. "Tell me," Bri requested gently.

"I came here to offer you comfort and friendship, not to beg it of you," Verena replied in a quavering voice.

Bri grinned. "Yes, you did, my dear. But you will see that whereas you took no for an answer, I will not. I am stubborn, so you may as well speak." Her voice softened. "And I can tell you need to."

"Oh, it's nothing, really," she said with a careless wave of her free hand. "I just have trouble talking about it."

"Why?"

Verena looked away again. Her voice was so low, Bri had to lean forward to hear her. "You know I was raped, Bri. I still have difficulty speaking of that time in my life."

Bri commiserated with her but said nothing.

Verena visibly brightened. "But that is the past and I have no desire to speak of it anymore. Adam Prestwich was the one that discovered the truth, by the way."

When she said the name, Verena watched for Bri's reaction. The countess stiffened for a moment before dropping a careful social mask in place over her features. Verena had been hoping for a way to casually mention Adam and judge for herself the way things stood between her two friends. Bri's reaction was not encouraging.

"Indeed?" Bri responded politely, releasing her hand and reaching for the teapot.

"Yes," Verena responded with false lightness.

Bri sat very silently. Verena wondered what was going through her head. The countess moved to set her teacup on the table in front of her. Her movements were slow as if she were moving in a dream.

The two women sat in silence for a moment. It was a tense, rather awkward silence fraught with uneasy thoughts on each side.

Verena was the first to speak. "Why, until today, have I been denied admittance?" she asked softly.

Bri threw her an apologetic look. She was unsure what to tell her without either hurting her feelings or letting on that she, Bri, was in trouble just as the marchioness suspected.

She chose her words carefully. "I'm afraid it was all a dreadful misunderstanding. My uncle, Corning, thought it would be painful for me to be reminded of that time when I was away."

Verena gave her an unreadable look. Her brow was furrowed slightly and she appeared to be thinking very carefully about the countess's words.

The silence returned. Neither lady even made a pretense of ease by reaching for a biscuit or refilling her teacup. Lady Rothsmere finally broke it.

"Why did you not approach me at any of the parties we have attended?" She sounded hurt. She could hear it in her own voice. She tried to smile but failed. She *was* hurt. Very much.

Verena reached out and grasped her hand. "I wanted to, believe me. But Connor and I thought perhaps you would not want to be reminded either. I know what a difficult time you've had since you left us. And then, of course, you were always surrounded by so many gallants, I didn't like to break up your enjoyment." She paused and bit her lip.

"What?" Bri asked, seeing her friend wanted to say something but was unsure if she should.

"Why Steyne, Bri?" she blurted out finally. "I mean, he was a scoundrel when I knew him and I doubt he's changed so very much."

"He is my betrothed," Bri responded tightly. "I am marrying him. That is an end to the matter." She rose, signaling the end of the visit. "I really must return to my other guests, my lady. Please excuse me."

Bri swept from the room with her head high. But Verena had caught the blaze of raw anguish in the depths of her friend's emerald eyes just before she had turned away.

Lady Connor Northwicke departed deep in thought.

# Chapter Twenty

Oh, it was all too much, Bri thought again as she tried to stop the perpetual flow of tears. She had noticed the hurt look on Verena's face when she had left yesterday and she hated having to hurt her. But she couldn't let anyone know of the perfectly miserable hell her life had become.

Brewster had proven to be a ruthless protector since the night of Bri's rape and the countess was eternally grateful to the woman. But there was only so much the woman could do and she couldn't be everywhere at once.

Bri shuddered as she remembered Steyne's visit in the middle of the night. He had been furious when Brewster had adamantly refused to leave her mistress's side—the woman had taken to sleeping in Bri's room at night. Steyne had left swearing retribution but even he knew the power of servants' gossip, so he had left with little more harm done than the threat.

Except the new bruise that Bri sported on her upper arm and along the outside of her right thigh. These had been acquired when the viscount had grabbed her arm and thrown her against the bed. Her leg had struck the bedpost and she ended up on the floor gasping and struggling not to cry. Her refusal to show her fear seemed to enrage him all the more and she had found herself being shaken roughly before her maid stepped in to put an end to the abuse.

That was when the viscount had taken himself off. Then Bri had once again found herself wrapped in the comforting arms of her maid and sobbing out her hurt and anger at the injustices of life.

Sunlight came through the part in the curtains and landed full on Bri's sleeping face. She came awake slowly, reluctantly. Her eyes opened, bloodshot from the tears shed in the night, with dark circles under them. A walk, she thought groggily, pushing herself up and out of the huge bed. She needed a walk in the fresh air, in the park, before anyone else was there.

Brewster came in and stopped short at the sight of her. Bri was wearing a nightgown of demure length but with no sleeves and made of near transparent white muslin. It was unusual for a young unmarried lady to wear such scandalous nightclothes, but Bri preferred it. Until now, that is. The maid's eyes widened in dismay and Bri looked a question at her before following her gaze.

"No," the young woman said determinedly, squeezing her eyes shut and clenching her fists against the onslaught of fresh tears. "I will not cry. He does not have that power over me."

And so she smiled brightly, despite the purple and blue bruise marring the delicate flesh of her upper arm and the soreness of her right leg. She had little doubt she would find it just as colorful. Brewster said nothing as she helped her mistress into a long-sleeved walking dress of dark blue. But she couldn't keep the pity from her eyes.

The sun was shining just as brightly as it had been when she awoke. Bri paused and lifted her face to the warmth of the sun just after they entered Hyde Park. Brewster waited patiently with a resigned look on her plain features until they resumed walking.

The women walked sedately forward, the maid a few paces behind her mistress as was proper. Bri longed for someone in whom she could confide. Only Brewster knew the extent of her troubles.

But there was little a servant could do. They could have Brewster killed—and, no, Bri did not feel she was making a Cheltenham tragedy of the situation or seeing villains were there were none—or make her conveniently disappear. They were in London, after all, where the East End teemed with seedy characters trying to make a living in any way, however disreputable, that they could. Disposing of a disobedient maid would be child's play to them.

Upon reaching a bench, Bri sat with an unladylike plop. She had never really cared very much for all the proprieties anyway. Brewster stood behind her.

"Sit down, Mary," the countess commanded softly. "I have need of your calm good sense."

The maid hesitated. "It wouldn't be proper, my lady."

"Hang the proprieties!" she exclaimed irritably. Then she

untied her pretty straw bonnet, removed it, and threw to the ground beside her.

Brewster pursed her lips in disapproval and thanked the fates that the park was even more empty than usual this morning.

Bri scowled up at her. "Sit, Brewster, or find new employ," she growled lowly.

"Well, put that way," the maid said with a faint smile. She sat.

Silence prevailed for several moments. Bri sat and listened, entranced, to the peaceful, calming sounds of birds trilling, the occasional bark of a dog, and somewhere beyond the park gates were the sounds of men and women hawking their wares to the early risers of London.

She sighed. "Why cannot life be simple?" she asked wistfully.

"Probably because simple is boring, I dare say," replied an amused voice behind her.

Bri swung around, eyes wide with fright, and encountered the serious blue-eyed gaze of Lord Connor Northwicke. His lips smiled but she could tell he wasn't truly amused at all. His eyes were blank.

"Lord Connor, how do you do?" she inquired politely. She rose to her feet and winced slightly as her injured leg protested the sudden movement. Brewster rose as well and curtsied before stepping a respectful distance away from the pair.

Connor caught the look of pain that streaked Lady Rothsmere's face. He said nothing, knowing instinctively that she would lie about its cause. Instead, he smiled and bowed before gesturing that she be seated again.

Brewster read a command in the marquess's eyes and walked a short distance away. Bri watched her go with a little look of dismay twisting her lips. She really did not want to be left alone with Verena's husband.

Connor sat down beside her, picked up her bonnet, and laid it carefully on the bench on his other side. He leaned back, crossed his arms over his chest, and stretched his legs straight out in front of him with his ankles crossed. He then proceeded to stare at his boots. He didn't look at her or speak.

"What brings you to the park at this early hour, my lord?" she asked with a bright, albeit nervous, smile. She realized she betrayed her nervousness in the way she fiddled with the ribbon of her pelisse and forced her hands to be still.

"Why does anyone walk early in the morning?" he replied with a shrug of one immaculately clad shoulder. "To commune with nature, to find a modicum of peace in an otherwise hellish existence, if you'll pardon the expression." He didn't look up. His boots seemed to be the most interesting things he had seen in quite some time.

Bri wasn't fooled by his apparently relaxed pose. She could feel the tension that seemed to radiate from him. He was waiting, biding his time. When he felt sure she had relaxed her guard, he would pounce. And she would be powerless to stop herself from telling him everything.

Fixing him with a steely glare, she intoned softly, "It really is no use, you know."

He turned a look of polite inquiry on her, blue eyes wide and innocent.

"Everything is fine," she lied. "I don't know what Doll told you, my lord, but—"

"Con," he said with a cheeky grin that she found thoroughly exasperating.

"Con, then," she conceded. "Whatever she told you, she's wrong."

His grin disappeared. He looked very…pensive, Bri decided.

"It wasn't Verena's very relevant worry that brought me here, Bri. It was actually what Miss Emerson told me."

"Miss Emerson?" she asked, startled.

"Yes, my dear Lady Rothsmere, Miss Raven Emerson. It seems she has taken quite a liking to you and has taken it upon herself to keep an eye on you. She's worried. She shared her worries with me. I am asking you if I should be worried about you."

Bri bit her lip to keep from crying out that she needed and wanted his help desperately, that she was likely to die without it.

But she said none of this and shrugged carelessly instead. "Any troubles I have are of my own making and trifling, I do assure you."

Well, she lied just as he had assumed she would. He watched her rise from the bench, retrieve her bonnet, and walk away with her jailer of a maid walking closely behind.

He had dropped Raven's name because he knew that Bri was more likely to seek out that woman's help before she would ever seek out Adam.

Which reminded him, Adam was due to arrive at his London residence later this day at the earliest. And if Connor knew Adam, he was probably already there.

He was. And pacing furiously in Connor's study. Verena was actually there with him, despite the queasiness of her stomach. She watched Adam pause, mutter something under his breath, rake a hand through his hair, and continue pacing. Her stomach protested and her head began to ache.

"Sit down, Adam, do," she commanded irritably.

He stopped and cocked an imperious brow at her. She pursed her lips. "Don't try to use your haughty look on me, Mr. Adam Prestwich, because I'll not have it. I know you're worried. I know you're restless. You are also making me ill. Please sit."

Adam grinned suddenly. Verena marveled at how very good-looking he was when he smiled. He didn't hold a candle to Connor, of course, but he was still very attractive.

He sat in the chair opposite, his grin never faltering. "You're increasing again, aren't you?"

Verena frowned in disgust. "Is it written on my forehead? I swear everyone knows and I've told no one."

An imp prompted Adam to inform her, "You are so moody when you are *enceinte*."

Her mouth dropped open in astonishment. "I am not," she denied fiercely. Then she smiled. "Perhaps I am, a little," she conceded. "Okay, a lot," she responded to the look of patent disbelief on Adam's face.

"I wondered if you were already here," Connor remarked to Prestwich as he entered the room. He bent to kiss his wife on the cheek. "And irritating my wife, I've no doubt. Did she tell you our news?"

"No, I guessed," Adam replied with a grin. Connor laughed.

Verena glowered at both of them. "Enjoy your jest, you great oafs. I am going to retire for a few more hours. I was only here to ensure Mr. Prestwich didn't break anything with his incessant pacing and grumbling. Excuse me."

"Was she this ill and crotchety last time? I was only present for the last few months, you know, and she didn't seem quite so tetchy although she was far more irritable than normal." Connor looked at the door and waited for his friend to answer.

A shadow crossed Adam's face. It had been an unusual situation. Adam had been present in Verena's life for the first five months of her first pregnancy instead of her husband. Con and Verena had actually lived apart just after the identity of her rapist had been discovered. So Adam had spent those five months traveling back and forth from London to the Dover coast in Kent where Verena had been residing with Con's Aunt Amelia. He was also using that time to search for Bri.

"Of course she was," he said now. "She may have actually been worse," he added thoughtfully.

Adam suddenly changed the subject. "Tell me what has happened to Bri."

Connor sighed, sat down in the seat just vacated by his wife, and shoved a hand through his golden curls. Adam raised his brows at this gesture. The situation was serious, then. Connor did not have the habit of shoving his hand through his hair unless he was very agitated indeed.

"I'm glad Verena chose to leave and I didn't have to force her to go," his friend commented much to Adam's surprise. The marchioness was usually completely in her husband's confidence. "The situation is far more serious than I revealed in that letter, Adam. Far more than any of us think, I'd wager. The trouble is, Bri won't talk to anyone about it. Not even Doll."

"She won't talk to Verena?" Adam echoed numbly. He felt suddenly very cold and a tingle of unease crept up his spine and into his brain to take up permanent residence there. "If she won't talk to your wife, her only friend, than who will she talk to?"

"Your mistress, I hope," Con replied. He looked at Adam and smiled faintly. "Sorry, she's not yours anymore, is she? Greville's mistress, now, from what I hear."

"Who the devil is Greville?" Adam asked.

"Bri's cousin and the only member of her family that seems to give a damn," the marquess replied shortly. He rose to his feet and retrieved the brandy decanter and two glasses.

Adam's brow furrowed. Her cousin? He couldn't remember meeting any cousin with any sort of filial affection for the girl. He met Viscount Breckon, nobody by the name of Greville.

He found a glass thrust into his hand and looked up into Connor's troubled face. The marquess sipped thoughtfully at his brandy and stared straight ahead. Then he set his glass aside and sat again.

"The thing is, Raven thinks Bri's been raped and fairly recently, too. Oh, I say—"

He leapt to his feet and pounded Adam helpfully on the back who had begun choking on his drink. Adam jumped to his feet, shook off his friend, and roared, "*What*?"

"Nothing will be solved if we get irate," Connor replied in a tone at odds with his recent agitation. "Raven said a week ago that she has been watching the countess and there were certain things she noticed. She said one or more of Bri's family members is keeping her in line with regular beatings. She also said it was very likely that she has been raped at least once by Steyne."

"I'll kill him," Adam said very calmly. His eyes held a look of steady concentration and deadly intent. Connor could see the man was serious. And that if he truly planned to kill the viscount, not a force on earth would stop him.

"We can't go into this half-cocked, Adam. We need a plan, a solution." He paused and regarded Adam with an expression that he couldn't like. He knew what was coming before the words were even spoken. "The easiest thing would be for you to marry her. Then you are in control and her family can do nothing."

"It's not as easy as that and well you know it, Con. Her family owns her until she's twenty-five. Over four more years. She must have their permission to marry and her betrothed must have their approval. If I took her to Gretna, it would not be difficult to prove the marriage groundless in the English courts especially with two dukes, an earl, and a viscount backing the decision. Besides," he continued, looking away, "I can't legally marry anyone."

"Whyever not?"

"I am already married."

# Chapter Twenty-One

Connor stared at him for a full minute in stunned silence. His reaction was not what Adam had expected. Actually, Adam wasn't sure what he had expected. He had never planned to tell his friend of his monumental foolishness.

So after staring for a full minute with a very blank expression, Adam was totally taken aback by his friend's explosive reply.

"The devil you are, you miserable bastard!"

Adam's eyes widened, his dark brows flew up into his hairline, and he unconsciously leaned back in his chair to put more space between their bodies. Connor's face was twisted with rage. He was at a loss to understand the marquess's reaction.

"Who the hell is she? Anyone I know? Is she a splendid baronet's wife, Adam? How many more secrets have you kept from me? Do I know you at all?" The marquess paused, seemed to shake himself, and then he quaffed his drink and poured another.

Then he understood. He almost sighed in relief. Connor was just hurt. He thought Adam didn't trust him enough to confide in him despite their years of friendship. He felt slighted, betrayed.

Betrayal. Oh, dear God, Adam thought numbly, all the color draining from his face. He remembered that look of betrayal in Bri's eyes that day in her drawing room. And he remembered the look in Verena's eyes when she came face to face with the man that had raped her only to learn exactly who he was.

*I almost feel sorry for Steyne.*

*You will not blame me for your own stupidity.*

Oh, what had he done? Had he really said those things to a girl who had just been raped by the very man sworn to protect her? Had he actually sided with the bastard? And then told her it was her fault and her problem to solve?

Connor was still glaring at him as he rose to his feet and left the room. He encountered Samson in the hall. The butler bowed and waited for Adam to speak. It was as if the man knew he would ask something.

"I need to see Lady Connor, if she is willing to speak to me," he finally stated in an emotionless voice. He was looking at the old man but he didn't appear to see him.

"What do you want with my wife?" Connor demanded in annoyance. He stood in the doorway behind his friend.

"I have to talk to her. Alone. It's important. Please."

"Alone? Whatever could you have to say to my wife alone?"

Adam sighed hugely. "If she chooses to tell you afterwards, so be it. It is up to her."

Connor stared for a long moment before nodding silently.

The marchioness presently appeared above them on the landing. "You wanted to see me, Adam?" she asked sleepily.

Prestwich bowed. "If you would be so good, my lady."

Her dark brows rose at his formality. She tossed a look of inquiry at her husband who shrugged. "Very well, sir. The library?"

Adam nodded and mounted the stairs.

"Bri—"

"No, Levi." The countess held up a staying hand. She removed her bonnet and handed it along with her pelisse to the footman. Then she walked by her cousin, intent on escaping to her room. Her morning with Lord Connor in the park was all the pressure she could handle just now.

Greville caught her arm and forced her to follow him into a little used morning room. It was the same room where Bri had entertained Verena and normally she would have found it a very pleasant place to be with the sun streaming through the windows and the general cheeriness of the décor. But the reminder of her rudeness to her only friend was depressing.

The countess winced when her cousin released her. He had taken her by the upper arm when he had grabbed her and she had actually forgotten the bruise there until he let go. It amazed her that she could forget. Perhaps she was becoming used to the beatings, she thought in a detached sort of way.

"How are you?" Greville asked solicitously.

"Annoyed," she replied tartly. "What do you want?"

The earl smiled. He leaned back against the mantle with one ankle crossed over the other and his arms crossed over his chest.

"Prickly, are we?"

"I don't know, are we?" she threw back sarcastically.

Greville pushed away from the mantle and approached her. He studied her very closely. "Raven says you're being beaten. Are you?"

"Raven says?" she asked incredulously. "Raven says?" Her voice rose in pitch. "Who the bloody hell cares what Raven says!" She spun away from him and stalked to the other side of the room. "Is Raven now the expert on my life? Does she know my every thought, my every action? Does she know?" She spun back to face him.

Lord Greville saw the emotions flit across her face. He saw the anger, the fear, and the panic just below the surface. He saw the way she darted fearful little glances at the closed door. He saw the fearful little glances she darted at him. And he noticed the way she favored her right leg and her arm where he had so recently touched her.

He swore, fluently. Bri's eyes widened at his inventiveness. Then a tiny giggle escaped her that quickly turned into a sob. Greville was across the room in two quick strides and gathering her into his arms.

"Shh, love," he murmured, rubbing a comforting hand down her back. "Everything is fine. I'm here now, love."

The countess jerked violently from his arms and punched him in the chest. "Everything is not fine!" she screamed. "Everything is not fine!" She pummeled him with her fists, she even kicked out at him.

"Stop it, Bri!"

She ignored him and he tucked her securely under one arm, went to the door, threw it open, and looked into the face of Mathers, the butler.

That worthy was startled enough to exclaim, "Oh, good Lord!" before his professional blank mask slipped into place.

Greville ignored the man's astonishment. "Send for Lord Connor immediately. Tell him to bring his wife and Prestwich if he has arrived. And send the countess's maid here. Now!"

The butler bowed and strode away as Greville closed the door, locking it behind him. Bri was still screeching like a banshee and trying to do damage to his person. He greatly feared for her sanity.

He took her by the arms and watched in stunned silence as her scream of anger turned to cries of pain. Great fat tears rolled down her wan cheeks. He released her, sliding his hands up to her face. "What have they done to you, Bri?" he whispered sadly.

There was a knock on the door. Greville pushed Bri gently into a chair and moved towards the door. He unlocked it and pulled it open, expecting the maid to be standing on the other side. He cursed when he saw who it was.

It was Steyne.

"You are alone with my fiancée, I think."

Greville just barely controlled his burning desire to beat the man to a pulp. "You'd best leave, Steyne, before I forget I'm a gentleman and I beat you right here in front of my cousin," he growled.

The viscount took a startled step back. Brewster appeared then and moved swiftly around the two men. Greville slammed the door in Lord Steyne's face, locked it again, and turned to the countess.

"What happened?" Brewster asked as she gently rocked her mistress in her arms.

"You tell me," Greville said. "Who's been beating her?"

"Who hasn't, my lord," the maid retorted softly. She brushed the damp hair from Bri's face and murmured something to her. The countess nodded, sniffled, and buried her face in Brewster's shoulder.

The Earl of Greville stood staring at them helplessly, battling his rage and wondering what he could do to help his poor mistreated cousin. He wanted more than anything to kill every bastard who had dared to lay his hands on her in any way. A sudden thought occurred to him that made him pale considerably, swallow against a fury that threatened to consume him, and pray for some semblance of control.

There was another knock.

Greville went to the door and threw it open again. Mathers bowed and announced in a wooden voice belied by the concern in his eyes, "Lord and Lady Connor Northwicke, Mr. Adam Prestwich."

*"NO!"*

# Chapter Twenty-Two

Lord Connor pushed his wife and friend into the room, shut the door, and locked it. The fury that was the Countess of Rothsmere launched herself at Adam and gave him the same treatment she had given the earl only moments before. Adam crushed her against his chest, pinning her arms harmlessly at her sides. When that didn't stop her banshee-like wailing, he did the only other thing he could think of.

He kissed her.

Bri stopped screeching so Adam let go of her arms, which she instantly wound around his neck. Then she kissed him back with all her heart.

The rest of the room's occupants just stared at them in surprise. Everyone appeared unsure what to do. Greville was clearly too shocked to leap to his cousin's rescue, as he should have done when a strange man took such liberties with her person. Connor was thinking that Adam really shouldn't be getting the girl's hopes up when he was married since it was painfully clear that she returned his feelings at least in part. Verena's thoughts were much along the same lines. Except, knowing more details about the marriage than her husband did, after her private chat with the man, she found herself wondering if Adam would kill his wife so that he could marry Bri.

Adam finally drew his head away from the countess, saw the drowned look in her eyes, and whispered for her ears alone, "I probably shouldn't have done that."

And, to everyone's considerable shock, Bri smiled. It was a smile of pure happiness. "No, you probably shouldn't have," she replied equably. "But you did."

Adam was very nearly lost in a world that contained only the two of them. She was playing with the little hairs at the back of his neck and smiling up at him with such trust and...love...that he could barely think straight. He brushed away her tears with one long finger, then drew it down along her jaw and kissed her again. Very lightly, like the touching of butterfly wings.

Connor cleared his throat and the two broke apart suddenly. Adam saw Bri blush and very nearly did the same himself.

Damn.

This meeting was not going the way he had imagined or hoped or even feared. He had been a trifle surprised to be accosted by one of the countess's footmen when he had left Connor's. Well, dumbfounded with shock would be more accurate, actually. The man had been clearly agitated and barely intelligible.

Adam had surprised himself by his patience. Instead of curtly ordering the man to spit it out and let him get on his way, Adam had instead encouraged the young man to breath deeply and concentrate on what he was saying.

The message had been a shock. After telling the man to return to his mistress, Adam climbed the front steps of Vale Place for the second time that day. Samson informed him that the marquess was in his wife's sitting room and offered to let his lordship know of Mr. Prestwich's arrival.

Adam had ignored him and took the steps up to the third floor two at a time. He knocked at the door of the room that he himself had just recently occupied with the marchioness and waited impatiently for an answer.

Connor had appeared in the doorway with a look of annoyance that had turned quickly to surprise and then to alarm when Adam informed him of the footman's message.

It had taken only moments for Verena to get ready and they were soon mounting the steps of Bri's home.

Adam stood back as the countess lowered herself back down on the sofa next to a tall, homely woman he assumed was her maid. Bri avoided looking at him and allowed the maid to hold her hand and listened attentively while the woman whispered something in her ear.

Lord Connor watched the scene for a moment with a grim expression before turning his gaze on the earl. "Care to explain?" he asked with raised brows.

Adam noticed the very large young man for the first time. He looked at him curiously and a trifle suspiciously. This must be the cousin, although Connor had not mentioned that Greville was such a giant.

Verena seated herself on Bri's other side and placed a comforting arm about her shoulders. She murmured things to her that were too low for anyone to hear and the countess was soon nodding and shaking her head at intervals.

Adam sat down heavily on a chair when his friend pushed him into it. He sent him a bewildered look but stayed put.

Connor indicated that Greville should be seated as well. The gentlemen's chairs were far enough away not to disturb the women and close enough to still know what was happening.

"I'm just so tired," Bri whispered to her two listeners. "I fight, but I know not what I am fighting against. Control, slavery, pressure, hatred, I don't know what is happening to me." She dropped her face into her hands and wept silently while Lady Connor and Brewster patted her back and murmured reassurances to her.

"What the devil is going on?" Adam finally bit out in frustration. "A footman nearly runs me down in the street and proceeds to tell me in garbled English that his mistress is in sore distress and needs Con and Verena and I to attend her immediately. The order was given by his lordship, the Earl of Greville. I assume that's you," he said as he looked at the giant, "and then we arrive to find the countess in a state of near insanity."

"You are Prestwich," Greville replied unnecessarily and with a definite edge to his voice. "Interesting. You're the reason she's in the state of mind she's in. I hope you're proud of yourself."

Adam edged forward in his seat. He ignored Connor who was trying to catch his eye. His anger with himself was taking control and at this point, he didn't bother trying to stop it. He didn't want to, in fact.

He smiled unpleasantly at the earl, his eyes as icy as his voice. "Call me out, Greville. I'm itching for a fight, you know."

"No one is going to challenge anyone," the marquess inserted firmly before Greville could take Adam up on the offer. The earl had a gleam of interest in his eyes at the prospect that Connor couldn't like. "We are going to try to determine what is best to be done since we are all on the same side here."

"Are we?" the earl asked belligerently. His angry glare was still directed at Adam.

"Yes," Lord Connor replied sternly. "More than you know," he added under his breath.

Adam sent him an odd look and Connor knew his friend had heard the comment. He chose not to enlighten him. "Do you stay here, Greville?"

"Yes, for now," the younger man replied, eyes still hard with anger. "Someone has to protect her now that she has been returned."

"Protect her?" Adam bit out contemptuously. "Is that what you call allowing her to be beaten and raped? Protection? You have a very odd idea of protection, puppy. Had you the sense God gave a flea, you would have killed Steyne by now. In his sleep if you had to."

He hadn't realized he was standing until Connor shoved him back down into the chair none too gently. He hadn't realized his voice had risen until he turned his head at the collective gasp that issued from the three women on the sofa. Then he cursed, fluently.

With another color epithet, Adam stood up and left the room. Steyne had the misfortune to be crossing the hall at that moment with a rigidly angry Duke of Corning and a slightly disdainful and annoyed Viscount Breckon.

Without conscious thought in regard to his actions and possible consequences, Adam closed the distance between him and Steyne in a few quick strides. Before the man could utter a word or so much as a blink, Adam leveled him—and then shouted at him to get up when the viscount remained seated on the floor with a hand to his broken nose.

Two large footmen rushed forward at the duke's command and took Adam by the arms. He shook them off easily since they actually didn't think he would try and punched Steyne again as that man had risen to his feet and was standing precariously with the assistance of Lord Breckon. Breckon caught him as he fell and held him up. The footmen meanwhile had managed to grab the baronet again and actually hold him this time.

At the duke's gesture, the men hauled Adam into an antechamber and stood in the middle of the room, still holding him tightly until the duke gave them the order to release him. This, he did not do.

The Duke of Corning strode forward and looked Adam up and down with a mocking half-smile on his face. "To what do we owe the pleasure of your presence, Mr. Prestwich?" he asked pleasantly. "Certainly you have completed your mission. My niece is returned to me, somewhat the worse for wear, but returned nonetheless. I can see no further reason for your presence in my home. I await an explanation."

Adam resisted the urge to spit in the bastard's smug face. He mocked him back, his stormy eyes hard as granite. "If I recall correctly, this is Lady Rothsmere's home, Corning. You are merely here on sufferance."

The unexpected jab hit Corning where he was most sensitive, his reliance on his niece's money for his creature comforts. The duke reacted purely from anger. He punched his prisoner with enough force to snap Adam's head back. The footmen had to tighten their hold on their captive to keep Adam from leaping on the man.

The duke rubbed at his smarting hand and continued to stare at Adam with cold contempt and mockery. "What has the little bitch told you, Prestwich? That she is mistreated? That she is being beaten for no reason? Believe me, that little whore deserves every bit of punishment she receives."

Adam had never before seen red. He did now. The efforts of the footmen were in vain. Adam made them release their hold on him by the simple expedient of cracking their skulls together. They slumped at his feet and he stepped over them. He was on Corning before that man even realized what was happening.

A second later, Adam was pulled off the duke by Greville and Lord Connor. Although, Adam reflected as he came out of his rage and beheld the bruised and bloody face of the duke, it may have been a bit longer than a second.

"That was a very bad idea," Connor muttered after Corning had been taken away by the butler and the duke's valet and the two footmen had been removed as well. "I will have a hell of a time keeping you out chains for this, Adam."

Adam turned a look of surprise on Connor. "Why?"

"Why? Have your wits gone begging? You just beat a duke, Adam. Attacked him in his own home. You won't stand a chance if he wants to press charges over this, you know."

"He won't," Adam and Greville said at the same time. They looked at each other with lowered brows for a moment before returning their attention to the marquess.

Greville explained. "The duke is very particular about appearances. He will not take Prestwich to court because of a broken nose. Steyne might, but I doubt that, too. Corning won't. He will come up with some explanation for anyone who needs one and glare haughtily at those who don't. Then he will seek to put Prestwich in his place in the only way he knows how: he will hire someone to kill him."

"That's rather barbaric, don't you think?" Adam asked dryly.

Greville shrugged. "It may well be, but it's also true."

Connor stared at both men intently. "What do you suggest we do, Greville?"

"Why do you ask him?" Adam asked with a jerk of his head in Greville's direction. "Don't tell me you believe this nonsense about Corning's trying to kill me?"

"I didn't say I believe it. However, out of the three of us, Greville knows Corning the best. And really, Adam, you should not be taking such a personal interest in Bri's problems. You know you shouldn't."

Greville looked from one man to the other, his curiosity evident in his dark eyes. "What's this?"

Adam ignored him. "I think you should mind your own affairs, Northwicke," he said very softly. "I will do what I feel I must. And I will not let Carly's existence stand in my way."

"Who is Carly?"

Connor and Adam turned at the same time and favored Greville with the same look. It seemed to consist of surprise that he was even there mixed with astonishment that he would ask such a thing with a little bit of threat thrown in for good measure. Greville thought it was a perfectly reasonable question considering his cousin was also a critical part of the conversation. And so he told them.

Adam, who had had his back partially to the earl, turned fully around and gave him a haughty look. "I don't see how Carly concerns you no matter what other lady we happen to be discussing, Greville. Carly doesn't matter, never has, never will."

"But she matters very much, Adam," Connor inserted firmly.

Adam released a sound of frustrated annoyance. "Devil take it, why are we discussing this right now? For all I know, Carly is dead by now and will cease to plague me."

# Chapter Twenty-Three

Bri felt ashamed of her behavior. She had not planned to attack anyone; she had definitely not meant to kiss anyone. But she had done both, barely remembering the one and thoroughly enjoying the other.

Damn him.

"My dear, it is surely not so bad as to warrant such tears."

Bri sniffed and looked up at Verena. She sniffed again, blew her nose into the large gentleman's handkerchief she held, and gave a watery chuckle. "No, it's not. I'm just so ashamed of myself. And now I've gone and dragged you into this and it's not your problem."

The marchioness favored her with a stern look. "It most certainly is my problem now, for I make it so. And Con will not allow them to treat you in such an infamous manner. Neither will Adam."

"Adam can go to the devil," Bri muttered.

"I'll not have you talking about him in that way, Brianna Derring," Verena replied with an edge in her voice. "He is putting more on the line for you than you can ever understand."

Bri glanced at her friend in surprise and annoyance. "When did you become his champion? I seem to recall him treating you as little better than a servant despite your marriage to his best friend."

"That's true. But things have changed and we all need to forgive when the time comes. And sometimes even when it doesn't."

Bri looked down at her tightly clenched hands. Then she glanced at Brewster who still sat beside her. "Mary, will you go get a tea tray, please."

Brewster nodded and left the room.

Bri stared at her hands again while Verena watched her friend. The countess looked terrible, Verena realized suddenly. Her eyes were puffy from weeping and there were dark circles under her eyes that suggested she had had little or troubled sleep for several days at least. Her hands were twisting the handkerchief she held beyond recognition. And she winced every time she moved her arm a certain direction or shifted in her seat. She wore dark blue, which was unusual since Bri tended to favor bright, shocking colors. Even her hair appeared duller than usual.

Her perusal was interrupted by the return of the gentlemen. Connor and Lord Greville preceded Adam who sported a split lip and a bruised jaw. The ladies started to their feet in concern but the marquess stopped them with a raised hand.

"I have asked your maid to pack your trunks, Bri. You are staying with Doll for a few days. Your uncle cares too much for appearances to make a fuss about it. Or so I'm told." He quelled the protest that rose to her lips with a glance. "If it will make you feel better, Verena needs you to be with her right now. She is expecting, you see."

Bri turned to her blushing friend, her look of amazement transforming into excitement. "Indeed? Oh, how wonderful!"

"Yes, well," Verena murmured with an embarrassed grin.

"And never have I beheld a more cranky woman than Lady Connor when she is *enciente*," Adam inserted with a wide grin.

Verena scowled at him. "What would you know about pregnant women, Mr. Prestwich?"

"Carly had one once," he replied without hesitation, a deep glare transforming his already harsh features into something positively satanic.

"Who is Carly?" Bri asked with a confused look. She looked at Greville.

"Don't ask me," he replied with a shrug. "I have been trying to discover that for the better part of a quarter hour."

"Is Brewster ready yet?" Verena asked.

"Who is Brewster?" Adam asked.

"My maid," Bri replied. "I imagine she will be here momentarily. How did you convince her to obey?"

"Convince her?" Con asked, perplexed.

"Yes. She is hired by Corning, after all."

"She is?" said Adam. "Are you sure? She seems completely devoted to you, my lady."

"My lady?" Bri murmured with a half-smile. "Why the formality, Mr. Prestwich?"

Adam's face went blank. "Formality is essential to my sanity," he replied dryly before turning away and exiting the room.

"Adam will tell you in his own time," Verena replied to the look of bewilderment on her friend's face. "Let us leave. I think I hear Brewster now."

He hated it when Connor was right. And he usually was, blast him. The marquess had finally managed to talk some sense into Adam before leaving the room where he had been taken by Corning. By the time they joined the ladies, Adam had agreed to keep his distance from Lady Rothsmere.

He wanted to do anything but. Just remembering the taste of her was enough to arouse him. Even four days after the fact. Damn.

Adam sat at the piano in the music room at Lockwood, tapping out a tuneless melody, while Morris poured him a drink. The valet was mumbling something unintelligible and Adam found he couldn't concentrate on any of his current problems.

"What the devil are you grumbling about, Morris?" he snapped irritably. "I can't hear myself think with your jabbering."

The valet released a few louder grumbles and directed them at his employer.

"You do, do you? Well, you can take your opinion and go to the devil, Morris. I have no need of them."

Morris rumbled something else, his own temper rising.

"Stubble it. I'm not listening," Adam retorted petulantly.

Adam nearly jumped when Morris suddenly shoved his grizzled head in front of him and let loose a series of grunts that Adam had no trouble interpreting as some very colorful expletives.

"I am not a child," he said defensively, sounding exactly like the very thing he protested being. He modified his tone before continuing. "Morris, unless you wish to find other employment, cease badgering me."

To Adam's amusement, the valet tossed his hands in the air, made a rude gesture to his master, and walked to the door.

"Morris, wait. If you want to go to Cornwall, fine. But I am promising nothing, old man. Carly is Carly and always will be. I don't believe women can change despite everything Miles says or you believe. But, we will go." He sighed expansively.

He really didn't care what Morris thought. Miles could harp at him for all he was worth and it still wouldn't matter. Adam would never change his mind about Carly. She was a viper and a schemer and he had no use for her. He would go to Cornwall for a time to appease his blasted servants and then he would return to make sure Bri remained safe from her family.

He didn't have much doubt on that score, however. He knew Connor would protect her with his very life if the need arose. And Verena was a veritable lioness when her loved ones were threatened. Bri would be fine.

There was also the arrival of Denbigh to Town. Connor had summoned the duke the day after Bri's removal from her uncle's care. Connor had been worried over the possibility of Adam's being taken up for attacking the Duke of Corning and had asked his father to lend his support should such an action come to pass.

Adam seriously doubted it would. Corning and his wife were so wrapped up in appearances that they had actually hired Adam to find their niece rather than call in the professionals of Bow Street. Adam grimaced in self-disgust as he thought about how he had unwittingly helped add to Bri's grief.

But had it really been so unwitting? She had told him, after all, what she had been through at their hands. Good Lord, she would have rather died than be returned to them. What a blasted fool he was.

Adam rose to his feet to prepare for the evening. He had agreed to attend a musicale that evening at Lady Denbigh's just across the square. The only reason he had agreed was because Raven had actually been hired to perform. It was something she had just recently started to do in order to more easily keep an eye on Lady Rothsmere. Adam appreciated everything the woman had done for him and wanted to show his support.

It had come to his attention that she had a new protector. He had been surprised to discover it was Bri's cousin Greville. After some minor detective work, Adam had found that the man had a small yearly income and he had trouble living within his means. Adam meant to ask Raven about that tonight.

Electing to be unfashionable and walk, Adam left the house. He made it about four strides when he was grabbed and dragged into an alley.

Bri sat between her cousin and Verena. She tried to concentrate on the music but her mind insisted on dwelling on the absence of Adam Prestwich. He had promised to be there, Verena had said. And he wasn't. The music had started nearly two hours ago and there was still no sign of him. And it was unlike Adam to be late especially to a party being given by the woman who was more a mother to him than his own had ever been.

Looking around again, She noticed her cousin Viscount Breckon watching her with a predatory look that made her shudder. Steyne was beside him with a smug look on his face. Bri wondered what they were up to. They looked far too pleased with themselves.

Why were they even there? She highly doubted they had been invited. Breckon may have been since he was still considered acceptable by even some of the highest sticklers, but Steyne was barely acceptable anywhere.

Especially now. His penchant for rape had somehow become the latest rumor. Apparently, he had had his way with the daughter of a merchant who had no qualms about taking the viscount to task for it. Steyne had become an anathema to the *ton* even though as a group, they openly despised those that made their money through hard work rather than inheriting it or marrying it. It was somewhat odd that they had chosen to side with the merchant.

Something was very wrong. She knew deep down that something serious had happened to cause such looks of satisfaction.

She relaxed when she saw the Duke of Denbigh himself approach the two men she had been studying and personally escort them out. She turned her attention back to the beautiful Miss Emerson.

The butler entered and approached Connor. After a few whispered words, a look of alarm crossed the marquess's face and he stood abruptly and followed the man from the room.

Something told her it had something to do with Adam. Bri muttered some excuse to Verena and Greville about searching out the ladies' withdrawing room. Then she hurried after Connor.

Traversing the darkened hall, Bri tried to keep Connor in her sight. She was unfamiliar with the layout of the mansion but it was much like others in Town, she realized with relief. She was surprised when Connor and the butler went up the stairs to the third floor where the family's private rooms were.

They stopped before a door about halfway down the long hall. Biggles, the butler, said something too low for Bri to catch, the marquess nodded, and the butler turned the handle and pushed the door open. Both men entered, leaving the door slightly ajar.

The countess hurried to the door, holding her Pomona green skirts well above her ankles. She peeked through the crack in the door and listened. All she could see was Connor standing with Biggles by the bed in the center of the room. She couldn't tell who was in the bed and the men's voices were too low for her to make out what was being said.

Connor turned and she beheld the grim expression on his face. Her worry increased. What was happening?

Biggles raised his voice enough that Bri could hear. "Should I send for the doctor, my lord?"

"No," Connor replied thoughtfully. "I will tend him myself. I think I know who is responsible for this. I don't want anyone to hear of this, especially the countess. Who found him?"

"It was Thomas, my lord, the knife boy. He was running an errand for cook when he saw three men drag him into the alley."

Lord Connor nodded. "Have a word with the boy. Emphasize the need for silence. I want Adam's enemy to think he is dead. It may be the only way to save his life."

Bri stifled her gasp. Oh, God, no! Uncle set those awful bullies of his on Adam and now he was barely alive. And it was all her fault, too.

She was so distressed that she missed Connor's next words. She crept away from the door, her hand over her mouth and tears coursing down her cheeks. She backed into a shadowed alcove and sat down. Con and the butler soon left, speaking lowly as they walked. They passed very close to her and Bri heard what they were saying.

"Under no circumstances is Lady Rothsmere to hear of this. I don't want her to…" Connor's voice trailed off as the two men descended the stairs.

Bri stared at the now closed door for a full minute. What if he died? It would be her fault. He had come to her defense and this was how he was to be repaid.

She had been told about his attack on her uncle. She had been shocked speechless that he would leap to her defense. But Greville had assured her that it was indeed true and that Adam had been marvelous.

And now he was dying. Or dead. Oh, what if he was already

dead? She would never be able to thank him for saving her life. She would never be able to thank him for defending her.

She would never be able to tell him how much she loved him.

She loved him. With all her heart. Life without him seemed dull and meaningless. Life without him would be utterly pointless. She realized she had actually loved him for some time. It had taken this horrible occurrence to make her mind form her feelings into words. She loved him.

And he was hurt.

Bri was at the door and turning the handle before she had quite grasped the idea to do so. She pushed the door open and walked into the room, closing it behind her with a soft click.

Lady Rothsmere approached the bed slowly, unsure what she would find and fearing it would be too much for her to handle. Her precious Adam was hurt and it was all her fault.

She stood beside the bed, her hands clenched into fists at her sides. She bit her lip to hold back the sobs of rage and despair. Silent tears streaked down her pale cheeks.

Adam's face was battered and bruised. His lip was split and puffy with a trickle of blood coming from the cut. She was sure both eyes would be swollen shut and black. There was a deep cut that started in the middle of his forehead and disappeared diagonally into his hair.

He was still fully clothed and lying on top of the bedclothes. She looked at his hand where it was lying over his stomach, two fingers quite obviously broken and swollen. She was sure he had broken and bruised ribs and possibly a broken leg as well.

Bri sat down on the edge of the bed and tried in vain to stop the sobs. They were too persistent, however, and she found herself crying as if her heart was broken.

And perhaps it was. Her only love was dying.

She reached out and very gently clasped his other hand, which was miraculously not injured, and held it against her chest. Leaning down, she brushed a soft kiss to his cheek. She started talking to him, hoping and praying that he could hear her, that he would understand and fight to live.

*"Adam, I love you. Please don't die. I can't live without you. You have to survive. You have to live so I can show you how much I love you. Please don't die."*

All this was said against his skin as she lay her head down next to him. Her tears bathed his neck and shoulder.

She was unaware of the passage of time. She lay there until someone entered the room and took her gently by the shoulder. She allowed this person to help her stand and lead her from the room. By this time, she was so numb inside with pain and fear that she was unaware of nearly everything around her.

# Chapter Twenty-Four

With a pain-filled groan, Adam Prestwich returned to the land of the living. He wondered if he was dying. His whole body felt as though he had been dragged behind a horse across the rocky moors of Cornwall. Naked.

He attempted to open his eyes. One refused outright and the other would cooperate only enough to allow him a very narrow view of the room he was in. He recognized his chamber at Northwicke.

What the devil was he doing at Northwicke? The last thing he remembered was stepping out of his townhouse with the intention of going to a party or some such nonsense and then…nothing.

What happened?

He tried struggling into a sitting position but was hindered by what felt like boulders pinning down his legs. A sharp pain shot up one arm causing him to cease attempted movement for the time being.

"Shh, Adam, love. Calm yourself."

He recognized Raven's husky voice. He tried to locate her with his one good eye. She appeared above him with a sweet smile. He nearly sighed in relief.

"What happened?" he asked with a grunt as he tried to move his limbs, which again protested vehemently. He groaned again.

"Stop, you'll make your injuries worse," Miss Emerson replied firmly. "You were set upon by footpads, my dear. Now rest."

Adam struggled to process what she was saying. It was difficult with the dull, sharp, and throbbing aches that seemed to completely consume his entire body.

"Footpads? Impossible. You must be jesting."

"Adam Prestwich, you need to rest. We will talk about this later." She paused and studied him worriedly, a very evident war going on behind her dark eyes. She seemed to come to some decision and continued. "You were beat pretty badly, Adam. Lord

Connor was unsure you'd live. He had no idea what internal injuries you may have sustained. The other physician he called had no better luck and less hope. Here, take this."

She shoved a spoon of some evil-smelling and foul-tasting concoction into his mouth before he had a chance to close it.

"Are you trying to kill me?" he asked hoarsely with a look of disgust on his handsome face.

Raven laughed lowly. "Of course, my dear. I am always out to kill, you know. Why not you, hmm? Perhaps you have left me something in your will, no?"

Adam groaned again to keep his lips from twitching into a smile and tried to fight the effects of the medicine that was rapidly putting him to sleep. He remembered an odd dream he had had while he was out and turned determinedly towards Raven.

"Where's Bri?" he asked on a mere breath of sound.

He saw her expression grow very worried, sad even. "She is with Lady Connor, Adam. She's fine. Now sleep."

The room grew very dark and Adam could no longer fight it. His last coherent thought before oblivion claimed him was that his ex-mistress was a terrible liar.

Bri was not fine. She was far from it, in fact. She was clinging to her sanity by a mere thread. Everyone was worried; no one knew what to do. Verena and Brewster were with her nearly every second of the day. She seemed to have slipped into a sort of void where no one existed but herself and her loss.

For some reason, everyone's assurances that Adam was fine, that he would live, wouldn't penetrate her depression. Connor wouldn't let her near the sickroom until he was sure Adam was definitely on the mend. Then he was unsure if it would be wise even then.

The countess sat for long hours watching the activity in the square. She had been moved to Northwicke along with Connor, Verena, and Greville. Her cousin tried to break through her defenses but he met with unwonted disappointment. Verena's twins had also been moved along with their nanny but even the delightful antics of the children failed to reach her.

It was Raven who succeeded in waking Bri from her trance a full week after the attack. She found the young countess at her usual spot in the drawing room, staring out into the square. Bri didn't even look up when Raven sat down next to her and very gently took her hand.

"Bri," the actress said softly. "Bri, you must listen to me, my dear."

Raven waited patiently until Lady Rothsmere turned vacant emerald eyes on her. "Adam wants to see you. He is asking for you. Has been for two days now, in fact." A light leapt into the countess's eyes. Raven frowned then, employing all of her acting skills to break through Bri's protective shell. "But I cannot allow it if you are going to be like this. He needs someone to cheer him. You, my lady, are not very cheery right now."

Something akin to anger flashed in Bri's emerald eyes. Then she opened her mouth and spoke for the first time since she had been pulled away from Adam's side.

"That was impertinent, Miss Emerson."

"Yes, it was," the actress replied with a pleased smile. "Will you see Adam now, my dear?"

"Of course."

Bri felt alive for the first time in over a week, no, in three years, when she entered Adam's room and saw him sitting up in bed watching her. His smile was all for her, she knew. She returned his smile and examined him with her eyes to reassure herself that he was, indeed, on the mend.

His one eye was still swelled partly shut but the other was wide open and alert. His broken hand lay motionless on the coverlet and his other hand was flexing restlessly beside him. He moved his body briefly and she caught the wince of pain that he wasn't quite successful in hiding.

She rushed to his side. "Oh, Adam, my love, are you all right?"

Adam grinned, ignoring the pain. "Your love, Bri?" he asked softly.

She stepped back, embarrassed. She remembered Raven suddenly and looked around self-consciously.

"She is gone. I asked to see you alone."

"Why?" she asked a trifle breathlessly.

Adam patted the bed beside him. "Sit and I will tell you."

Bri sat down next to him primly. She kept her back straight and tried to control her breathing. He was staring at her as if he was trying to divine her innermost secrets and it made her uncomfortable.

She appeared thinner, he thought. And somehow the shine that always seemed to surround her was missing. Her hair was a duller shade of the normally vibrant red and her green eyes were shadowed. Her dress hung like a sack on her. Where on earth had she found such an unattractive gown?

Adam pushed that thought aside and wondered what the devil he was thinking to ask to see her alone. He had no right to speak to her. It was dishonorable for him to do so. But he loved her. And he remembered her telling him that she loved him.

It couldn't have been a dream. He refused to believe it had been the mindless wanderings of his own fevered brain. It had to be real.

"Do you love me?" he asked her before he realized what he was even going to say.

She started. And avoided looking at him. "Why?"

"I seem to remember a green-eyed goddess telling me that she loved me and couldn't face life without me. I thought it was you." His eyes teased her. "Perhaps I was mistaken."

Bri took a deep breath and forced her eyes to meet his. Then she was trapped. She opened her mouth to speak but he words wouldn't come and she gazed into his helplessly until he finally broke away and fiddled with the coverlet, staring at his hand.

"Forgive me, Lady Rothsmere," he said stiffly. "I had no right to tease you so. Your feelings are irrelevant. As are mine."

"What?" Irrelevant? What on earth was he talking about?

Adam looked at her. Her emerald eyes were confused and her face held a hurt look. He sighed. "I can't speak, Bri. It's not honorable. I have…things to take care of before I can speak. I…" He trailed off and looked away from her.

*What is there to lose?* she wondered with a mental shrug. "Adam, I do love you," she whispered. "Tell me what prevents you from speaking the same words."

Adam took a deep breath, tried to think of some way out of his current predicament, and sighed when he admitted that she had to know. "I'm married," he finally said dully.

She couldn't breathe. It felt just like someone had punched her in the stomach. She saw the blackness threaten to engulf her and fought it back. She would *not* swoon! Of every possible excuse, marriage was not one she could have imagined.

He was married. "Do you love her?" she asked in a tiny voice.

"I have not for some time," he answered honestly. "But that does not change the fact that I am married. She is in Cornwall with my cousin Miles right now. I was planning to go there and see her because…well, because she's dying."

Bri felt very guilty for the sudden leap of hope she felt at his words. "I don't know what to say," she finally offered lamely. "You say you do not love her so to say I'm sorry you are about to lose her seems pointless. To be pleased about your imminent release is just evil."

"Yes," he agreed. "Miles insists she is not the same woman she once was. I have decided to listen to him for once in my life and return home to see for myself."

"I think you should," Bri offered softly.

"You do?"

Bri looked into his stormy eyes, read the surprised curiosity there and half-smiled. "Yes, Adam. I think there is some hurt in you that has everything to do with her. Perhaps if she has changed, you will be able to forgive yourself for abandoning her."

He started. "How did you know…?"

"It wasn't hard to determine," she said with a smile. "You showed your pain and distrust too many times for me not to notice. She did something to destroy your faith in women. You left her and have felt guilty over that ever since. It is time to absolve that guilt, Adam."

He said nothing and just continued to look at her. She forced herself not to fidget under his steady gaze.

"Who is Levi?" he asked abruptly.

"Levi?" He nodded. "You have met him. He is my cousin Greville. Did no one ever tell you his Christian name?"

He flushed. "No, no one ever did."

"What made you think of it?" she asked in amusement.

Adam stared hard at her and turned away before answering. "I have been jealous of him ever since the first time I heard his name."

"Whatever for?"

"Mrs. Campion told me you mumbled his name when you were feverish. I haven't been able to get rid of the urge I felt then to find out who he was and remove him from your life," he admitted with a rueful grin.

"Levi likes you, you know."

Adam raised one dark brow at her.

"He does. Told me you were a great gun. I called him a traitor," she admitted teasingly.

Adam's good humor fled. His face turned grim and tortured. "I am sorry for that, Bri."

Bri lost her own smile. "For what?" she asked very quietly.

"For not believing you. For returning you to hell. For allowing them to do what they did. God, Bri, I am sorry," he ended on a shuddering breath, tears standing out in his eyes as he thought of everything she had been through because of him.

Bri reached out and took his hand. "You are not to blame, dearest. Truly. I may have been angry with you at first but I never understood. I understand now and I forgive you for not believing me. I am sorry for this." She gestured helplessly at his broken limbs. "I am to blame because you defended me. Forgive me."

"Listen to us," Adam said with a chuckle. "Begging each other's forgiveness for events beyond our control. Pathetic."

"Yes, quite," she agreed. She tried to release his hand but he wouldn't let go so she just held it tighter.

Raven popped her head around the door. She smiled at them. "Everything better?" she asked brightly.

"Come in, Raven," Adam invited with a smile. He released Bri's hand. "Did you need something?"

"I was asked to bring this to you," the actress replied.

She handed him a sealed letter. It was from Miles. Adam felt short of breath and afraid. What if she was already dead? Would he ever be able to forgive himself?

He cracked the seal and read the words. She wasn't dead, Miles said, but the end was very close. Adam leaned his head back and sighed. Then he held the letter out.

Bri took it from him with a curious glance sent Raven's way. That woman shrugged her delicate shoulders but said nothing.

Bri unfolded the parchment and read the brief note. She looked at Adam and studied his face. He appeared upset although his face was blank and his eyes were closed. His hand, however, was balled into a tight fist.

"Raven, will you send for Con please?"

# Chapter Twenty-Five

The men who had attacked Adam had been apprehended. Connor was satisfied with their punishment of transportation. He had yet to tell Adam of this latest development. He had already planned on visiting him with the news when a servant informed him that Lady Rothsmere and Mr. Prestwich were asking for his presence.

Connor entered the room with a smile on his face that quickly disappeared when he beheld the grim countenances of his friends. He sent a curious glance at Raven who curtsied and then excused herself and closed the door behind her as she left the room.

"What's to do?"

Bri rose from the bed and handed Lord Connor the letter she held in her hand.

"Read it," Adam commanded.

Connor did. His confusion increased. "What do you want me to say, Adam? That I'm sorry? This woman has put you through hell. And she is probably in considerable pain anyway."

"I have to go to her, Con. I have to talk to her again before she dies."

Connor threw a sharp look at Bri. She smiled. "I agree with him," she said simply.

"Are you asking me if you *should* go or if you are *well enough* to go?"

"Neither, actually," Adam replied, finally opening his eyes to look at his friend. "I am going. I was hoping you would go, as well. And Verena and Bri, of course."

"Is that wise?"

"Probably not," Adam admitted. "But I find I can't face her alone."

Bri stood impassively by the bed. Connor looked from her to Adam and back again. "Did you agree to this as well?" he asked shortly.

"This is the first I've heard of it, my lord," she replied gravely.

"I see."

"Do you?" Adam asked. "It would surprise me, Con, truly it would. Will you go?"

His friend stared at him for a tense moment. "Very well. Is there anyone else you would like to be there?"

"Raven and Greville," Adam answered instantly. "If Denbigh and the rest of your family have no problem with Raven's presence, invite them as well. A house party makes the thought of facing her that much more possible."

"My family had no problem inviting Raven to stay here," Connor replied dryly. "Gwen and Jenny like her," he added in reference to his twin sisters.

"Good. I wish to leave today."

Morris entered the room and grumbled at Adam. Adam laughed and told him to pack anyway and he could gloat later. Connor shrugged and bowed to Bri and took his leave.

As he walked through the door, he heard Morris grumble again and then Adam called Connor back.

"What?"

"Have you found them yet, Morris wants to know?"

"Oh, the devil, I forgot to tell you. The men who actually beat the tar out of you were transported yesterday. Father and I saw them off personally. And the duke has begun a plan to make Corning pay as well. It seems Corning has a few radical leanings that father thought the House would be very interested in learning about." Connor grinned. "He'll have to hole up on the continent to avoid the ramifications of certain actions that could very well be considered treasonous."

"There, Morris, you see? Nothing to worry about."

Bri cast an amused look at Connor who returned it. Then he left.

The party that descended on Adam's residence in Cornwall consisted of Connor's entire family, Bri, Raven and Greville. Miles was shocked but bore up under the strain very well. He wished Adam had written to warn him of all the extra people.

His cousin's appearance was also a shock. He held his tongue until they were alone and then listened in open-mouthed astonishment to his employer's tale of revenge.

"How very Gothic," Miles commented dryly. "Are you sure you weren't just set upon by footpads?"

Adam gave him such a speaking look that Miles chuckled. "Very well. I believe you. It was revenge. But why the sudden house party? And in the middle of the season, no less?"

Adam shrugged. He looked down into his glass of brandy as if the answer might be hidden somewhere in the amber depths. Then he sighed. "Perhaps because I'm still a coward."

"A coward?" Miles scoffed. "You?"

Adam looked at him with carefully blank eyes. "I've always been a coward, Miles. I run from my problems instead of facing them head-on. I try to pretend that they no longer exist instead of trying to solve them. I'm a coward."

"There is a difference between being a coward and being scared, Adam," his cousin retorted softly. "You're here now and that's all that matters right now. You are planning to see Carly?"

Adam nodded. He couldn't trust himself to speak. He wanted to tell his cousin and everyone else to go to the devil and leave him be. It was easier to run, he had convinced himself long ago.

Except, now it wasn't. There was Bri.

"I will see Carly," he replied finally. "But not yet. I'll let you know. In the meantime, have Raven attend her."

"You know, Adam," Miles said uncomfortably, "it's not good *ton* to bring your mistress into your home."

Adam finished off the liquor in his glass and set it aside, grinning. "Oh, Raven's not my mistress." Miles sighed in relief. "She's Greville's," Adam said with a chuckle as he left the room. He was rewarded with a groan from his steward.

Raven did as she was bid and went to meet her new patient as soon as possible. The day after their arrival, in fact. It had been more difficult than she had imagined it would be. Greville had, for some reason, taken exception to her acting as nurse to Mrs. Prestwich.

"You don't have to, Raven," he had commented from the doorway of her chamber when she was preparing to go to Adam's wife.

She turned around. "Of course, I do, Levi. Mrs. Prestwich needs care. She's beyond the doctor's help now."

"I mean," her protector retorted as he entered the room and

closed the door firmly behind him, "you do not have to obey Adam Prestwich anymore. He has no hold over you now."

Raven had laughed. "He never did, my dear."

"Are you purposely misunderstanding me?" Greville groaned in frustration. "I don't want you jumping to do that man's bidding, Raven. I won't have it."

Raven straightened to her full height—which wasn't much shorter than Greville. She fixed a steely dark-eyed gaze on him. "*You...won't...have...it?*" she said slowly and distinctly. Her eyes flashed dangerously.

Greville had never seen Raven in a temper so he hastened his own death with his next words. "Of course I won't."

"Who the devil do you think you are, Levi Greville? I'll tell you who you are," she answered herself as she stalked up to him, her hands balled into fists on her hips. "You are my protector, chosen by me, and nothing more. I don't need a protector; I had planned on not taking another one after Adam. So, do not"—she shook an admonitory finger in his face—"tell me what I will and will not do!"

And then she had stormed from the room.

Now, as she entered the Rose chamber allotted to Adam's wife, she wondered if the earl would drop her. It tore at her heart to even think about it. She was very much afraid she had fallen in love with the impossible young man.

Raven was, once again, playing her role of governess. Her hair was scraped back into a bun and her dress was plain to the point of severity. She bustled into the sick room with all the confidence of her breed.

As she neared the bed, Raven smiled brightly and said, "Hello, Mrs. Prestwich" before she had gotten a good look at the woman in the bed. When she finally took in her appearance, Miss Emerson, the Ebony Swan, gasped and lost all of her carefully cultivated aplomb.

Adam's wife stared as well. And it was no wonder, Raven thought sympathetically. The woman had probably just reached the same conclusion she had. It was like looking in a mirror. Adam had been much more attached to his wife than he had let on. He had taken a mistress that could have been her twin.

# Chapter Twenty-Six

Nearly a week after his arrival, Adam requested Miles to present him to his wife.

Miles was surprised by this request. It was made humbly and with some hesitation, maybe even fear. Adam appeared to be quite upset but not in the way Miles would have thought. He looked almost sad.

Upon entering his wife's chamber, Adam felt a sense of unreality. It had been well over two years since he had seen her, longer than that since he had married her. She looked up at him from the big bed with the wide amber eyes he remembered so well. They had always reminded him of warm honey.

Lady Carlotta Prestwich greeted her husband in a voice that was low and husky like Raven's. He realized with a start that Carly was like Raven in many ways. They had the same black hair, the same low voice, the same graceful carriage, and the same height and shape. The differences were actually small. The eyes were different and Raven's hair was very straight where Carly's was a riot of curls.

Was, anyway. Now her hair was dull and lank. Her eyes were still bright but there was pain there, too. Her frame was emaciated. He felt very sad that her beauty was so far gone.

He tried to dredge up some of the anger that had sustained him through the years but it was gone forever. He was only sad now.

He approached the bed and sat down beside her. "Why did you do it?" he asked softly.

The woman in the bed fought the tears and lost. They poured down her cheeks and her lips moved soundlessly. He reached for her hand and squeezed it gently. This action seemed to increase her distress and Adam began to worry that she might worsen her condition if she didn't stop soon.

"Carly, you must calm yourself. I have no desire to see you do yourself harm in this way," he murmured. "Please calm yourself."

Carly valiantly tried to stifle her tears. She finally succeeded. In a broken voice, she said, "Why did you never ask me to explain then?" Her voice was slightly accented and thick with her tears.

"I was hurt, Carly, obviously," he replied with a tinge of sarcasm. "Why Steyne? I could have dealt more easily with anyone but him."

She blanched. "You don't know, do you?"

"Know what?"

She tried to answer but her frail body was wracked by a violent fit of coughing. Adam procured a glass of water for her and lifted her up to drink. He was reminded of another young lady he had helped in just such a way and was surprised at the feeling of tenderness that he actually felt for this woman who had betrayed him in the worst possible way. She swallowed the water, thanked him gravely and tried to shrug out of his embrace. He wouldn't let her.

"Tell me what I don't know, Carly," he commanded gently.

"Very well, Adam." She shifted slightly against him until her cheek rested against his chest. "The first time with Steyne was my fault, I admit. I was seduced by his words and empty promises. But I realized how very much you loved me and tried to break it off. He threatened to kill you or me if I left him. So I stayed. And when you found us, I saw the look on your face and knew you would leave. I was glad. I wanted you to move on with your life, to find somebody worthy of you.

"I admit with shame that I developed an addiction to opium as a way to cope with my sorry life. It was that habit that nearly destroyed my little Calandria."

"Where is she?"

"She is here, Adam. She is installed in the nursery with your old nurse. She is three years old and walking and talking as much as her mother was wont to do. I am so sorry, Adam. Can you forgive the stupidity of a lonely and selfish girl?"

"I was not a very good husband to you, Carly. I should have talked to you instead of assuming you were with him out of choice."

"I was with him out of choice in the beginning, Adam. I was one of those females you hated. I was greedy and opportunistic. I treated you badly and you deserved so much better."

"Carly, you are dying," Adam said after a few silent moments.

"Yes," she replied. Her voice was a mere thread of sound.

"Do you forgive me for leaving you?"

"Yes, Adam," she breathed. "But only if you will forgive me for my unfaithfulness."

"I forgive you."

"And my lies, Adam," she added.

"What lies, sweetheart?"

"About Callie."

Adam felt his heart skip a beat. "What about Callie?"

But Carly didn't answer. Her breathing grew labored and her hand tightened spasmodically on his arm. He seemed to feel her slipping away from him. He wanted desperately to know what she was about to tell him about her daughter.

"Carly, love, tell me about Callie," he commanded hoarsely. "Carly?" He shook her and raised his voice. "Carly?" But he knew it was already too late. Carly was dead.

Adam directed Miles to make funeral arrangements. He also informed his cousin that he would be taking care of Carly's daughter. Miles had sent him a perplexed look but agreed nonetheless.

Everyone avoided Adam until the day of the funeral. He had been so pensive, so thoughtful that no one had wanted to disturb him. He would wander around the house, ride out on the moors, and sit at the piano in the music room, displaying a talent that no one had even suspected.

Bri would have worried if she hadn't sensed that he was at peace within himself despite his odd silence. She assumed he had had a chance to talk with his wife before she died and she was glad. He had to put his feelings of guilt behind him if he were to achieve any sort of happiness in his life.

Adam didn't realize all the speculation he was causing. He was too lost in thought. She had been about to tell him something about Callie. She said she had lied. He remembered her telling him during one of their many fights that the baby wasn't his. Was that the lie? Dare he hope?

He found it too painful to hope for that. And he couldn't bring himself to visit the little girl. He had told Miles at the funeral that he wanted the child to stay but she was to be kept from his sight. He just couldn't bear to see her and find that she looked just like

Steyne.

Thinking of the viscount caused a spasm of rage. Damn, but he should have killed the bastard when he had had the chance!

He was sitting at the piano one day playing in a desultory fashion when the doors opened to admit Bri. She paused on the threshold and just stared at him. He just stared back.

How much time passed in this fashion was anyone's guess. But suddenly, Adam was standing stiffly and Bri was hugging him as if trying to disappear into him. He hugged her back, ignoring the stiffness in his leg and the soreness of his ribs.

"Talk to me, Adam," she said against his chest. "Tell me what has you wandering the house like a specter. Tell me what happened before Carlotta died."

With a sigh, Adam walked over to a sofa in the corner. He lowered them onto it without releasing her. He actually lifted her and settled her in his lap. She made no protest, cuddling into him instead.

He told her in a low voice all about his marriage, how it was Steyne who had been with his wife, how the bastard had tricked her, and how Adam had abandoned Carly to her fate along with her unborn child. He told her of his very last meeting with his wife, how she had died in his arms and despite the fact that he had not loved her the way she needed, a part of him had still died with her.

When he explained Carly's last words and how she had been unable to tell him what she had lied about, Bri sat up and stared at him in amazement.

"Do you mean you have not been to see little Callie yet?"

"No," he replied. "I couldn't bear the thought of her looking just like Steyne."

"Oh, my dearest," the countess breathed. She leaned forward and touched her lips to his briefly, very gently. Then she smiled. "Come with me, Adam."

She took his good hand and led him from the room, up the stairs and to the nursery on the fourth floor. When he realized where she was going, he held back.

Bri stopped and wrapped her arms around his waist. "Do you trust me, Adam?" She asked gently.

"Yes," he said without hesitation. And he was very surprised to realize it was true.

"Then come with me. As soon as you see Callie, you will see

what I saw and all your worries will vanish."

Her words did not reassure him but he followed her anyway. The nurse stood up upon their entrance and curtsied awkwardly.

"Master Adam, my lady, what can I do for you?"

Adam's brows lifted at the woman's greeting and then he smiled. She had been his nurse when he was a child and he had actually not seen her for many years. Probably close to twenty-five, in fact. She still looked exactly the same as he remembered her.

"Is Callie awake, Mrs. Bowers?" Bri asked.

"Yes, my lady," the old woman replied with a smile. "And expecting you for the past hour. She is in her room getting something she wanted to show you."

"Wonderful." Bri smiled. "Adam has come to make her acquaintance."

The old woman nodded and smiled. "I will leave you alone with her then, my lady." She curtsied again to them both and left the room.

"Is this really necessary?" Adam asked his beloved. "Cannot you just tell me what it is I am about to discover?"

Bri smiled enigmatically and released him. She crossed the room and disappeared through a door on the other side. After a few moments, she returned with a very small, black-haired girl in her arms. The little girl giggled at something Bri said and Adam found the sound enchanting even though he tried desperately to harden his heart against the pain he knew was coming.

Then they were before him and Bri asked him if he would like to hold her. He noticed the child looked down at her hands the whole time. He shook his head.

"I insist," Bri said happily as she switched Callie from her arms to his. He took her reluctantly and glared suspiciously at Bri. That young woman just grinned in obvious delight.

"Sir Adam, allow me to introduce you to Miss Callie Prestwich. Your daughter."

Adam sent her a half-angry look. She smiled brightly, completely calm. Then she redirected her attention to Callie. "Look up at your father, dear."

Callie lifted her head and Adam gazed into eyes the color of a storm washed sea. They were wide and bright, gray-green just like his own. And she was the spitting image of his youngest sister. He felt a lump form in his throat and he had to swallow hard against the threat of tears.

He failed miserably. Hugging the little girl to him, he cried even as he smiled. Bri cried too and he gathered her to him as well.

"Thank you," he whispered to no one in particular.

# Chapter Twenty-Seven

Callie was quickly a favorite among Adam's guests. Connor and Verena's twins were delighted by the company in spite of their being so much younger. Verena was delighted with another child to mother although she never overstepped what she considered Bri's authority. Bri had already fallen in love with the child even before introducing her to her father.

Connor's sisters, Gwen and Jenny, spent nearly as much time in the nursery as Bri and Verena. They were nineteen and everything to do with children was their secret delight. Raven visited often but she was usually found in company with the duchess, which was a surprise to everyone except Connor and Denbigh. Greville was young enough to find children somewhat bewildering and more than a little annoying. So he spent most of his visit with the duke discussing everything from politics to farming.

Adam, who now used his title since Verena had accidentally let Bri in on the secret and that young lady insisted that he use it, tried to stay away from the nursery. But his steps invariably led him there. He would stand in the child's room while she was sleeping and just stare at her in wonder and regret the lost years with her.

He was glad he had come home to see Carly before she died. A great weight had lifted from his shoulders. He knew even after her apology that he had never really been in love with her. His love for Bri seemed to make his feelings for Carly pale in comparison.

He had not yet discussed with Bri his feelings for her. He wanted to marry her more than anything, immediately, but he was unsure of himself and her. He should be in mourning for his dead wife. And he was, actually. But Carly had told him that she had wanted him to move on years ago. Carly had known that he had moved on. How could she not?

A few weeks after Carly's death, Adam's guests decided it was time to return to Denbigh. They included Adam and Callie in their plans to leave as well as Bri and Greville. The twins insisted that Raven be included in the invitation and were so persistent that Lady Denbigh finally agreed just to have a little peace. It helped that the duchess was impressed with Raven's air of gentility, as well. Adam went along with their plans as he had ever since the death of his wife. He offered no argument, no resistance, and no complaint. He just went.

His reaction worried everyone. Adam was no longer the cynical, sardonic Adam that everyone had come to know and love. He seemed to have retreated into himself and no one knew what he was thinking since he refused to talk to anyone.

The twins thought that perhaps he had loved his wife very much indeed and didn't want to face life without her. Connor wondered if Adam's feelings for his wife had been stronger than he had thought. Verena was a little closer to the truth. She thought Adam carried a feeling of guilt around him like a shroud and instead of forgiving himself for whatever action it was he was ashamed of, he wallowed in it. The duchess was inclined to stay out of Adam's troubles and Bri was just too worried about him to do aught else.

Everyone hoped that things would change upon their arrival at Denbigh Castle. Unfortunately, after placing his daughter in the nursery under the care of the loyal Mrs. Bowers, Adam retreated to his apartments and was rarely seen by the other occupants of the castle.

A family meeting was called. The only ones absent from the gathering were certain uncles, aunts, and cousins who knew nothing about the situation and honestly didn't want to know. Even Dr. Steele had been called in, having known Adam nearly as long as the rest of the Denbigh's.

Everyone offered up their opinions and carefully considered everyone else's before it was finally decided, a full three hours later, that the duke would be the best one to approach Adam and ask outright what was going on since he stood as a father figure to the baronet. He gravely agreed to do his best to sound Adam out on several issues, most of which he did not share with his family.

That this was Verena's suggestion gave that young lady a feeling of smugness that she didn't hide very well. She remembered several conversations with Adam and even her husband where more was discovered with forthrightness than hedging around the real issue.

The Duke of Denbigh found his might-as-well-be-adopted son sitting at the piano in the vast music room two days after the family meeting. The duchess and Miss Emerson were off somewhere on the estate and his daughters were with Lady Rothsmere and Verena in the nursery. Greville was visiting the doctor, with whom he had developed a rather unexpected friendship. Connor had gone with him.

Denbigh entered the room silently and sat down to listen. Adam played with a feeling for the music that seemed to communicate his feelings more accurately than he could verbally. He played a somewhat sad melody written by someone unknown to the duke at this particular moment. It was sad and yet it wasn't. It seemed rather…resolute, final…accepting.

Adam stopped before he had finished it. His hands remained motionless on the ivory keys. Without turning he said, "Did you want to talk to me, sir?"

Denbigh stood and approached. "I have been asked by my duchess as well as others to find out when you plan to marry that girl."

Adam looked up and regarded the duke with an amused smile. "I'm sorry for that."

Denbigh sat down on the bench beside him. "Well?" he asked as he started to pick out a tune on the keys.

Adam laughed. "Well what?" he hedged.

Denbigh smiled. "It really is none of my business, as I told your adopted family. But they do insist. How long have you played the piano?" he asked abruptly.

"Forever," the baronet replied laconically.

"How the devil did you manage to hide such a talent from your family?"

Adam smiled sardonically. "By family, I assume you are referring to yours." He shrugged nonchalantly. "Con may know, I am unsure. Does it matter?"

The duke ignored this to ask, "What were you playing when I walked in?"

"It doesn't actually have a title yet. It's not even done," Adam said with a rueful half-smile.

Denbigh stared at him. "You composed that? You are full of secrets."

"Not anymore," Adam answered mildly. "I believe you all know my best kept secrets now, sir. I have a title. I was married. I compose music when I need to escape. I play music when I need to think. Oh, and I have a child." He paused a moment before continuing. "Which happened to be a better kept secret than any of the rest since I didn't even know."

The duke chuckled and his hands stilled on the piano keys. "Yes, I know your secrets. Your daughter is a delight, by the way. She looks so much like you there is no doubt of her paternity."

"I know."

Denbigh studied Adam closely but the man's expression was unreadable. "So, are you going to marry Bri?"

The baronet laughed with self-deprecation. "I would like to, sir. More than anything, actually. But I doubt she'll have me."

"She will. She's just waiting for you to ask." He paused and glanced away from Adam's suddenly smiling face. He was a little unsure how to continue. Verena's words leapt into his head and he decided to heed them. He simply pointed out an obvious fact. "You have changed, Adam."

The smile disappeared. "How so?"

"I cannot recall a time when you were so thoughtful, so… unapproachable. Even when you were told of your family's demise, you were still the same old cynical Adam Prestwich. You brushed through that as if it had never happened and other than a caustic remark about the dilapidated state of the house and grounds, you had nothing to say about it." He looked over at his silent companion. "What has happened now?"

Adam sighed. Bri was the only one who knew of his discussion with Carly, although it was obvious that Denbigh had determined that there had been some doubt about Callie's paternity. He really didn't want to discuss it.

"Never mind, my boy. It was impertinent of me to ask."

"But you and everyone else are like to die of curiosity if I keep silent," the baronet remarked with a flash of his old cynicism.

Denbigh chuckled. "I will survive, Adam. Greville doesn't want to know although he does worry for Bri's sake and Connor is too conscious of his own secrets to probe where he is not wanted. The twins view you as another brother and my wife as another son.

Needless to say, Bri is worried. Miss Emerson worries but assures us that you will come around. I can't help but believe her since she seems to know you better than the rest of us. How she accomplished such a feat amazes me."

"The ladies are only interested in my intentions toward Bri," Adam inserted with a slightly derogatory sound.

"We're all interested in that."

"I'm sure."

A silence fell between the gentlemen that was neither comfortable nor uncomfortable. It just was. It lasted for all of five minutes before Adam finally broke it.

"I'm finally at peace. All this time, I blamed myself for my failed marriage and blamed women for my unhappiness. I have known very few women who have not proven to be scheming and manipulative. My own mother and sisters were of that cast." He paused, considering. "I don't deserve her, do I?"

"Perhaps you should let her decide that, hmm?"

"Perhaps," Adam agreed reluctantly.

"You don't think you should?"

"She has been through so much. I don't want to add to her pain anymore than I already have."

Denbigh regarded him silently for a moment. "Remember when you met Verena. You had every reason to believe that she was one of those typical women for whom you have every aversion. You held to this opinion until she confessed to you about her rape. Yes, she told me of that," he said in response to the surprised look on Adam's face.

"Where are you going with this, sir?"

"My point, Adam, is this. You were the one who knew what had to be done to save her. Do not let Bri's similar experience hold you back from making her happy."

The duke rose to his feet. "Think about that, lad." And he left.

# Chapter Twenty-Eight

Dinner that night was not quite the ordeal that Adam would have expected. Everyone talked and laughed and fervently ignored Adam's silence. They took turns drawing him out until he finally put his morose thoughts firmly in the back of his mind and concentrated on being a more congenial dinner companion.

In the drawing room afterwards, he played for his guests, allowing himself to get lost in the music. He thought of all that had gone on in the past few months and wondered if it was a good idea to marry Bri. It wasn't the thought of her rape and the fear of hurting her that actually held him back. It was something she had said to him nearly seven months ago. He had been unable to get it out of his mind ever since.

She was so bright and cheerful now that he suspected it was all an act. What was she thinking at this very moment?

Bri was actually pondering the sadness and melancholy that translated itself through his music. She didn't yet know that Adam was the composer and she wondered what he was thinking as he played. His expression revealed nothing. She couldn't see his eyes.

Would he ask her to marry him? Sometimes she thought he might not in spite of everything. She loved him now more than ever and was determined that they be together no matter what.

The piece drew to a close and Adam sat very still at the piano. Everyone else sat very still as well.

Then Denbigh, with a mischievous grin, asked, "What is that one called? I'm afraid I don't recognize the composer."

Adam looked up and smiled but didn't answer.

The company dispersed soon after that and wandered to their beds. Adam paced his chamber, much to the disgust of Morris, still fully dressed and muttering to himself the whole time.

He was fighting the urge to go and talk to Bri that very minute. He had come to the decision while he was playing earlier that he would ask for her hand and let her decide what was best. But he couldn't go to her room now. It was well after midnight. She would be compromised.

That thought made him stop in his tracks consideringly. Then he shook his head in disgust and continued pacing. He couldn't possibly be so selfish as to force her hand. But perhaps he wouldn't have to. He stopped again before he suddenly spun on his heel and walked out.

The countess sat in bed as still as a statue. Her hair was down around her shoulders and she was in a crisp white nightdress with long sleeves. She had stopped wearing her sleeveless ones ever since that morning when she had seen the bruises left by Steyne.

She shuddered at the memory. She was glad the viscount was firmly in her past although she was unsure if he had actually given her up or if he was merely planning something.

And then there was Adam. Would he ask her soon? She prayed he would. She wanted to be with him more than anything.

As if conjured by her thoughts, Adam appeared in the doorway and closed the door firmly but quietly behind him. She was suddenly glad that Brewster had taken to sleeping in the dressing room again.

"Adam? What is it?" She rose from the bed and approached him cautiously.

"I need to talk to you," he said. He watched her warily, noting that she was in her undress. He hoped she would have the good sense to keep her distance. He suddenly wanted her with an intensity of feeling that he had not experienced in a very long time.

"About what?" She halted a few feet away, all at once conscious of the fact that she was standing before him in her nightdress. She saw the heat in his eyes and felt a frisson of fear mixed with excitement course up her spine.

Adam thought about all he wanted to tell her, all he felt and wanted in his life. She stood before him expectantly, holding her hands loosely clasped in front of her. He wanted to touch her, to hold her, but knew it would be unwise.

She took the decision out of his hands. He looked down into bright green eyes when she laid her hand on his arm.

"Tell me," she whispered.

He reached for her hand, twining his fingers with hers and slid his other arm around her waist, drawing her against him. She watched his face wordlessly. Then he leaned down and kissed her tenderly, lips slightly parted. She pressed her lips back to his and opened for him in an invitation too tempting to resist.

She seemed to burn in his arms and it was only natural that he lift her and carry her to the bed. She held tightly to him when he tried to move away. His senses returned and he realized he couldn't take her now. He sat down beside her, smoothed the hair back from her face and smiled before gently taking her hand.

"I'll not make love to you, Bri. Not now."

"Why not?" she asked breathlessly. He saw the bewildered hurt in her eyes and was startled to realize that she actually wanted to be with him.

"Are you not afraid?" he asked with no small amount of curiosity and concern.

She swallowed hard but did not look away. "Yes," she answered honestly. "But you…you wouldn't…you…"

"I wouldn't hurt you," he said for her. "I wouldn't, Bri." His brow furrowed. "Well, I would try not to, anyway. But I actually came here to beg your forgiveness for putting you through so much hurt. I know saying I'm sorry isn't enough and if I could change the past, I would. But I can't so all I can do is apologize."

Bri hid her disappointment well. She leaned back slightly and tried to smile. She was afraid it appeared to be more than a little sad, however, when she replied. After taking a deep breath, she said, "Of course, I forgive you, although I really do not feel there is anything to forgive. I blamed you at first, it is true, but I have realized since then that you only did what you could at the time." She shrugged and looked down at her hands where they lay, linked, in her lap. "In fact, if you hadn't saved me when you did, I would have hanged as a common criminal. No matter what I've said to you in the past, I was at *point non plus*.

"And," she continued with barely a breath as she twisted her hands nervously in her lap, "I have decided that changing the past is not always a good idea. I would not change the past now since it has brought me you. If I had not run away, my family would never have hired you and I would never have met you. Or Connor or Doll. I have too many blessings as a result of my choices and I would not trade any of them. Not even to avoid the pain and heartache I've had to endure."

She looked up into his eyes then and determinedly shoved away the little voice that warned her to *not* utter the words that trembled on her lips. She knew deep down, she would regret it forever if she simply let him walk away with nothing more than her unwarranted forgiveness.

"I owe you something for your help, Adam. I'll do whatever you want."

Adam's eyes grew wide in shock but then his lips twitched suspiciously. He was laughing at her! How humiliating! It was obvious to even the greenest of girls that while Adam Prestwich may care for her, it was apparent that he did not love her or even want her enough to make love to her. She let her chin drop in dejected misery.

Adam smiled at the emotions that flitted chaotically across her lovely face. To think, he came here to offer her his heart and the propriety of a marriage bed and she seemed to be offering something quite different. He could not be mistaken in the invitation that had shown so briefly in her eyes.

He tilted her chin up with thumb and forefinger and looked deep into her eyes. They were awash with tears of dejection and humiliation. "If you're offering what I think you are, I have to decline," he whispered sincerely. Before she could react, he continued to talk as his thumb lightly traced her lower lip, causing a visible tremor to snake through her body. "As much as it may kill me to do so, I want to wait until we are married. That is, if you have changed your mind," he added sadly.

"Changed my mind?" the countess asked faintly. He had said they would be married! He must love her!

"You told me once that anything was better than spending your life with a man who had betrayed you. Do you still feel that way?"

Bri started. He actually remembered something that she had said several months ago. Something she had said in anger and fear. And now he was throwing it back in her face. Well, not actually throwing, but placing in front of her, anyway.

"Oh, I was so angry, Adam, when I said that. And at the time, I meant every word." She smiled at him hesitantly. "I have not changed my mind about it, either," she added honestly, because, in fact, she hadn't. She still felt it would be hell to be with someone who had betrayed her.

He reached out and stroked her cheek gently. "Then this is goodbye, is it not?" The softest of smiles touched his face and a look of intense sadness entered his pale eyes. He rose to his feet.

Bri reached up and took his hand, gripping it tightly. "You didn't let me finish," she said quickly, fiercely.

Adam sat again and squeezed her hand. "I apologize. Please finish."

"I would never spend my life with a man who betrayed me," she said softly. She clutched tighter at his hand—as if that were possible. He could barely feel it for lack of circulation as it was. "You have never betrayed me, Adam," she added emphatically. "You were always there for me, no matter what. If I could have let go of my stubborn pride enough to ask for help, I could have avoided nearly all my troubles."

Adam stared at her. The truth of her words blazed in her emerald eyes and he knew she truly did not believe he betrayed her no matter what he thought of the situation. Adam felt a smile tugging at his lips, a smile of absolute joy. "I have forgotten to tell you something," he said.

"What is that?" Bri asked in bewilderment. It wasn't exactly the reaction she had expected.

Instead of saying what he wanted, Adam kissed her. He communicated all his love and emotions in this one kiss until he was sure she understood. He wasn't disappointed. When he lifted his head, Bri was staring at him with those wonderful eyes of hers and she was crying.

"You love me," she whispered tremulously. "You actually love me."

"You will marry me, then, my love?"

And the Countess of Rothsmere smiled brilliantly through her tears and threw herself into his arms again. "Oh, yes! Yes, Adam, please, I will marry you!"

# The End

# Regency Romance by
# Jaimey Grant

***Betrayal***   ISBN 1440414688  Trade Paperback $9.95
ASIN: B001IKKMEA  Kindle Edition $6.95

Bitter and angry after the abuses she's suffered, Bri finds herself compelled to accept the help of a man she believes she loathes.

***Spellbound***   ISBN 1440414726  Trade Paperback $9.95
ASIN: B001IZZ2S6  Kindle Edition $6.95

When offered the most dangerous role of her life, retired actress Raven Emerson accepts, more than a little intrigued by the eccentric duke making the offer.

***Heartless***   ISBN 1440414742  Trade Paperback $9.95
ASIN: B001IZZ2RC  Kindle Edition $6.95

Abandoned and desperate, Leandra Harcourt agrees to marry a man she later learns is known as Lord Heartless.

***Redemption***   ISBN 144041484X  Trade Paperback $9.95
ASIN: B001J6N9LQ  Kindle Edition $6.95

Lady Jenny Northwicke's head is turned by a dashing rogue, resulting in scandal and ruin, betrayal and heartache.

Jaimey Grant loves to hear from her readers. For questions, information on upcoming releases, or signed copies, you can contact her at jaimeygrant@yahoo.com

Made in the USA
Lexington, KY
24 February 2010